AWAKENING
COCIJO

AWAKENING
COCIJO

THOMAS JUAREZ

ISBN: 9781093640588 (print)
Also available in ebook

Edited by Amber Byers, Tadpole Press
Cover and book designed by Sue Campbell Book Design
Author photo by Makenna Aitson

Contact the author:
 tom-juarez.tumblr.com
 tjuarez66@yahoo.com

PART ONE

CHAPTER 1

Lyobaa, Mexico 120 BC

L YOBAA, TODAY KNOWN AS MITLA, IS THE RELIGIOUS CENTER OF the known world for the Zapotec. A journey is about to begin, a pilgrimage to the great city on the mountain. A chance to demonstrate obedience to the gods, and to observe of the heavens. Danaà, the great seer, is the high priest; a man with all the wisdom, knowledge and power in Lyobaa.

"Make haste," he barked at his comrades, "the gods do not wait on men!"

Danaà, unlike any of the more common priests of the kingdom, is a mountain of a man. A priest of divine blood lines, he looked to be more suited for soldier duty than to that of the meditative duties performed by a holy man. He has a cleft chin, eyes darker and sharper than the black obsidian used for the crafting of weaponry, and an extremely muscular build. His wide, burly shoulders appear as though they could carry the full mantle of the gods.

"I'm moving as fast as I can, but Ayotli is moving so slowly, what am I to do uija-tào?" The young priest apprentice, Beedxe', giggled as he poked at his small and quirky travel companion. Danaà, the high priest of the Zapotec, also carried the title of uija-tào.

Beedxe' is only fifteen years old with wavy black locks and the face of a child. He speaks playfully with the little man, as the little man is simple and fun to be around.

Ayotli, as mentioned, is small in stature. What he lacks in size he makes up for in lightheartedness and laughter. His rosy red cheeks are highlighted by his never-ending smile. Smiles, he insists, are just as infectious as frowns; best to wear the face of merriment.

Danaà grinned and growled, "That is why we call him Ayotli ... slow and steady does it! These next days we move at his pace; it will take us two days, and we must harvest toloache for many things, your rite of passage to manhood among them, Beedxe'."

They watched in amusement as the little man fumbled around in a slow and steady frenzy, something they jokingly referred to as *turtle-like stealth*. Beads of sweat raced their way from the little man's forehead down to the tip of his chin; there forming large beads of liquid before falling to the ground below him.

Ayotli was named for a turtle, which was a fitting name for someone so slow. Also fitting that turtles were as green as the jade he masterfully shaped and polished. Jade was for the elites in society. It was only to be worn by those of divine ancestry; those whose ancestors descended from the clouds, and those who would one day return to the clouds upon their earthly passing.

Queen Zyanya was very fond of Ayotli's work, which made him a very beloved commoner and successful merchant. It was difficult sometimes for commers such as Ayotli to remember their place in society. Commoners could never become elite, as they were not descended from divinity. They could, however, improve their status among the common class of society. People with achievable goals were more apt to have aspirations worthy of an orderly community.

"I have designed many wonderful and astonishing treasures for our great queen: a necklace, a bracelet, and many stones I have prepared to please her senses and shine light in her eyes. I hope that she will admire them and shower me with favor as she has done before. Perhaps even take me on a hunt! There are few things that hold more excitement than the hunt."

The divine ones would often take deserving commoners on hunting parties. This was considered a great honor and earned them a better standing amongst those in their class. One could even find himself chasing a deer from the brush just in time for the killing blow to be delivered. As in many cultures, prized animals such as deer were reserved only for the upper crust of society.

"For you, uija-tào, I have crafted this necklace from the greenest obsidian the gods have ever created. My hands felt as if they were guided by Cocijo himself. Surely a descendant of the great god of lightning is meant to have such a treasure. I hope you find it pleasing and powerful. Best to keep cloth between your skin and the amulet, eh?"

Green and black stones adorned the chain of the necklace, making it appear commonly elegant enough for the great seer. At the base of the long chain, designed to adorn the mid chest, was a lightning bolt made of pure green obsidian. Green obsidian was more rare than the common black obsidian often used for weapons. When chiseled, obsidian became razor sharp and gleamed in any light.

"You honor me before our great journey!" Maliciously smiling, he grunted "If you were a woman, I would kiss you. Instead I give you this, you will need it today."

A freshly cut and carved walking stick! Surely this would be a fruitful journey! The rounded and beveled handle fit perfectly in his hand. The staff was ordained with the most eloquent fretwork Ayotli could have imagined; the ascending geometric lines jumbled and pleased the senses. It was almost a shame to use such a staff for walking the treacherous terrain they would face … almost.

"And for me?" Beedxe' wondered aloud feeling left out. "Someone has to have something for me, don't they?"

"Easy my young apprentice … could we leave here without gifts to honor your future bravery?" Danaà looked almost lovingly at his young pupil and raised a single eyebrow. "You are among the youngest of our village to ever become a priest. This is not to be taken lightly. I have two sacred pendants, which have been crafted and consecrated just for you. One is made of hessonite and the other of onyx. You must hold one in each hand during the oblation. Take good care of them, Beedxe'. Keep them safe."

The pendants resembled jaguar heads. Beedxe', after all, means jaguar, and he was born on the day of the jaguar. The onyx head was as black as the soil surrounding the obsidian mines, while the hessonite was a brownish orange. Both pendants were polished to a glass-like shine, truly a powerful moment for the young one.

"They're majestic! Do you think I will earn them?" There was a crackle in his voice that was part nervousness and part something else … perhaps doubt or immaturity.

"You WILL earn them!" Danaà retorted with a fist to his chest. "I am not in the habit of making false prophecies. I told our king as I told your father, you are a Nagual; do not doubt yourself Beedxe'. Your purpose, as well as your gift, will be revealed for all to see. The only question that remains is this: will you be a man who holds the jaguar within you, or will that man become the jaguar? Only the gods can reveal this … only during the alignment."

He gently placed his closed fist on the cheek of Beedxe', showing the testosterone-filled pride exhibited only by the most prominent men of the Zapotec empire. Then he offered "Soon … soon … you will see!" He looked into the boy's eyes as if projecting his own internal strength into him.

Gesturing with a wave of his arm "Now let's get going! Guards, we will follow the river. You will keep your distance, but you will ensure our safe passage to the city." Priestly conversations were not the business commoners or soldiers. Ayotli, though a commoner, served as jeweler to the queen and often served as a trusted travel companion to Danaà.

The guards turned, placed the base of their spears in the ground, nodded at one another, then began to march. Because they were not in a warring or ceremonial capacity, the soldiers wore simple sandals and loin cloths made from coyote hides. Any colorful paints worn may attract the attention of those looking for trouble, and this was a religious campaign.

"What are their names? There are only two, don't you think we should at least know their names?" said Beedxe'.

"No! This is a rite passage, not time to make friends. We must let them guide and protect us, this is accomplished by leaving them be. Warriors need not hear priestly mutterings"

And with that, they were on their way. While Lyobaa was located in a tropical and deciduous forest, they must cross a forest of pine and oak as well as desert-like terrain of the valley on their way to Monte Albàn. The trek would lead them though the varying ecosystems of the Oaxaca basin, each filled with its own natural beauty and danger.

High stepping through the deciduous forest outside their front door, Beedxe's eyes opened like a spring flower reaching for the sun. At fifteen years old he had rarely seen the lands outside the city walls. He had been protected since Danaà prophesized he would grow into a nagual. Nagual, also known as shapeshifters, are extremely rare, especially in the arid environment known as the Oaxaca basin. Their coming signifies great things were to come ... including possible signs from deities.

While signs and omens were not uncommon, signs of divinity were extremely rare. It was whispered that the gods would shine blessings upon the nagual, and an abundant harvest would follow. Though a ferocious and often warring society the Zapotec were, above all, dependent upon their agricultural prowess.

Danaà let out a rumbling bellow, a laugh carrying strength from the underworld itself. "Your eyes are bigger than the stars! We really should have let you wander outside of the walls more, boy." Kneeling down along a narrow part of the river, Danaà signaled for a hush. "Shhh ..." As if he had the capacity to hide that large frame, "Look."

The three of them knelt by the river as the guards halted and turned. Danaà pointed to the river's edge waving and shaking his forefinger. A lizard nearly two feet in length rested atop a large stone near the water. Brown, with a long yellow-green stripe from its eye to its tail, its head was shaped like an arrow tip. Ayotli smirked, winked and snickered as he clapped his hands. They all watched in amazement as the basilisk awkwardly raised his body to a semi-upright position and scampered across the water on its hind legs.

"They can run on water?" Beedxe' was so excited he almost yelled. Even the guards cheered in celebration of the majestic nature with which this creature moved. All creatures have spirits, and the spirit of the basilisk allowed him to tread water.

"There are a great many things you have yet to see my young nagual. What I really must know, is how they appear to you when you are one with the jaguar." Danaà genuinely wondered aloud.

"I will try not to eat it, bahahaha." Beedxe' let loose laughter that infected his comrades with silliness. "Perhaps I could eat something delicious, like a rabbit. I do not think Ayotli would please my appetite, he is way too skinny!" he said as he poked the giggling little man in his rib cage.

"I know in my mind that I am delicious, but please eat the rabbit." Ayotli rubbed his belly as if he had eaten something pleasant. "Let's get a sip of water and be on our way. There's much more to see. Carefully now, keep an eye out for snakes, they like to hide among the rocks."

Each of them knelt next to the water, closer this time, close enough for replenishment. Cupping their hands together they washed down a few guzzles, then splashed some briskly across their faces and through their hair. The water was clean, cool, and soothing to the soul; everything water should be.

"We will stop for a break later under the shade of the trees. Be vigilant, we are sure to run into larger animals than a basilisk in the forest." Danaà warned the entire group, gesturing to the guards to keep their eyes peeled. Wolves, foxes, coyotes, and ocelots were just a few of the creatures demanding their respect.

Again, the group marched on. As they walked, Beedxe' could not help but to think of the awkward, yet efficient way the little brown beast moved. This smile quickly dissipated as humor turned into concentration on the pace of their march. Their eyes were trained on the bounties and perils of the natural world which sur-rounded them; watching the sun bend shadows, seemingly making them dance. They looked attentively, watching, and hoping to see something exciting; an omen perhaps.

Walking … walking … and walking …

CHAPTER 2

After walking a couple of hours in direct sunlight it was rewarding to finally enter into the shade of the pine forest. Even the keenest of eyes needed a minute or two to adjust to the sudden deprivation of light. Called the pine tree forest for its rows upon rows of seemingly endless pines, it also contained many an oak, and the grandiosely imposing cypress. Shadows cast from these trees hid the sun, and often hid hungry predators.

"It is here we rest." Announced Danaà, motioning the others to have a seat on a collapsed tree. Convenient of the tree to fall just where they needed to sit and rest. "We will need to have our wits about us in the forest. Watching a deer bound by or admiring the conical beauty of flowers exploding from the bromeliad can give predatory beasts all the time they need to pounce. You may believe large predators will be easy to spot, but they would not dominate the forest without the blessing of stealth and, of course, natural camouflage afforded them by the gods. Also, we must watch the ground for snakes and such."

"Well, that makes me feel better," Ayotli nervously smirked and giggled. "You let me know if you see something young Beedxe', so I can run behind you."

"I bet you would! What happened to the spirit of giving?" Laughing along playfully, Beedxe' enlarged his eyes and pretended to be a small child in need of protection.

"Then I guess it is time I give you the obsidian blade I have packed for you. Don't get too excited, it's simple, not to be admired the way you would my jewelry; but be careful young one, it is very sharp!" Reaching into his bag, Ayotli removed a simple weapon as promised. "I used the antler of a brocket deer to mount the blade upon. The hilt is strong, and the blade is sharp, everything a knife should be. Keep it sheathed in this buckskin until you have use for it."

Beedxe' took a break from reality to admire the weapon and its razor-sharp edge. *Best be careful*, he thought as he walked to some nearby ferns to test the cutting edge. Amazing how effortlessly it glided through stem and leaf.

"A fine weapon! Sometimes I think you spoil the boy, but surely, he will find a use for this gift. I am impressed Ayotli, this is nicer than the meager blade you keep for yourself." Danaà pointed at the four-inch blade that never left Ayotli's hip.

"It is well broken in, a gift from our great king. I believe I told you of the large white tail I chased from the brush for him?"

"Yes, yes ... I was just having a bit of fun. I am capable of an occasional joke, you know?"

Smiling and bowing Ayotli proclaimed, "Of course, uija-tào. You are the great seer, can you not see my amusement?"

"Indeed. All the same, we have rested long enough and should be on our way." Danaà then turned to the guards and ordered the pace to be tempered down to an even slower pace. They'd need extra time to inspect the brush as they made their way through it. The importance of showing respect for the strength of animals could not be understated.

Danaà helped his approached his young apprentice, looked him in the eye, "Rested and ready, my young nagual?"

"Yes, uija-tào. The further we remove ourselves from home, the more I feel I am truly a kindred spirit to the animal kingdom. I intend to earn the title you have bestowed upon me. Your visions are known to carry the will of the gods, and I can feel a change. I can really feel it."

A look of stern encouragement consumed Danaà. It almost appeared as though tears of parental admiration formed in his eyes. The thought of Danaà raising a boy as his own was unheard of—priestly duties were meant to consume the daily life of an uija-tào. The great seer quickly whipped his head around. Forward, he motioned to the guards, waving in a circular motion over his head, and pointing at his eyes as if instructing the two men to keeps their own eyes focused on the terrain.

The pace, as instructed, was slower yet more deliberate. The forest came to life with curious creatures poking their heads out from everywhere. There were pygmy skunks (best to keep a distance), mockingbirds, hummingbirds and the smaller cousin of the ocelot, the margay. While margay are not big enough to menace men, it was a reminder that larger predators were afoot. Gray wolves, puma and the jaguar all possessed the power and skill necessary to hunt their small traveling guild.

The pine forest lasted only a short time as they came upon a large, very old cypress tree, which was rumored to hold mystical powers. All forms of moss, epiphytes, and bromeliads adorned the tree making it appear as though engulfed in the dreams of men.

The wonder before them seemed to create its own topiary. It appeared to be dozens of trees wrapped into one; some areas looked to ascend as brownish green columns while other areas of the tree were tall, flat, wall-like surfaces. At its base, it was the breadth of a small pyramid, and its roots burst from the ground eager to cast the entire forest in a dream-like trance.

"It is said that the great Pecala, god of dreams, placed this necromancing tree here to mark the passage into the valley," Danaà said, "though some have surmised that it is the earthly resting place of an ancient king."

"Something stirs behind it uija-tào," one of the guards warned while he pointed at the base of the massive tree.

"Beedxe', come here boy." Danaà was attempting to make his bearish voice whisper. "Where are the stones Ayotli crafted for you?"

The boy reached in his pack and presented the two jaguar stones, "I have them right here."

Stealthily advancing from behind the cypress as if summoned by the gods, the jaguar revealed himself and paused, eyes glaring at the men with deep hunger and controlled fury. Black jaguars were a rare sight, the strength they possessed was unrivaled in the known world of the Zapotec.

The cat growled and roared as if it were representative of an entire army of men standing their ground. Drooling and pacing beneath the tree, threatening imminent death to any brave or foolish enough to challenge. There would be no retreat from the beast.

"Close your eyes," Danaà said in a now still voice, instructing the inexperienced nagual, "feel his breathing, feel his hunger. Where men have fear, he has passion and power."

"I can see him!" Beedxe' said. "Even with my eyes closed I can see him! I feel drawn to him."

"You see! This is a sign! Now, open your eyes and move towards him. Slowly now." Danaà gently pushed the youngling on his way.

Beedxe' took slow, purposeful steps. He allowed his breathing to mirror that of the revered beast awaiting him. As the distance between the two lessened, a kinship seemed to build. Growls turned to silence, nervousness to confidence. He proceeded until he could feel and smell the breath of the great cat, which now beckoned him forward.

Beedxe' knelt in front of the beast, extending fisted hands clenching the jaguar stones; stones that Danaà said possessed enchantment and invocation from the great uija-tào himself. The beast snarled, releasing a thunderous clamoring of violent roars. Confidence now consumed the young nagual. He believed! He was Nagual, and he was now standing before the spirit animal sent to him from the gods. The snarling reduced to a grumble as the majestic cat circled in front of the curiously emboldened boy. Beedxe' thrust his fists forward again, gesturing for approval.

Placing its muscular head beneath the boy's right palm, the beast nudged the hand, making only a nasally snuffling noise as it continued to inspect the visitor. The cat grimaced and opened its mouth, seemingly preparing to attack, it demanded obedience. Beedxe' didn't dare move or show any form of weakness or fear. Satisfied, the beast snorted before turning and walking away. Beedxe' remained entrenched in his crouch until the creature was beyond sight.

The small conglomerate of men stood, dumbfounded, stunned in awe and amazement. They had witnessed a young priest's indoctrination into the spirit realm of the jaguar. He clearly *was* the nagual, and the prognostications of Danaà had become reality. The guards knelt and showed their loyalty, admiration, and their acceptance of the young nagual.

Beedxe' slowly turned and stood. Words need not be spoken. The boy was now a man, a man with the heart of a bewhiskered marvel. The rite of passage to be held was a mere a formality, manhood was earned in these times.

"We will make camp under the dream tree tonight. Guards! Gather wood and make fire! We make camp here tonight!" Danaà said as he turned to his young pupil, his eyes on fire. "You see? You have strength uncommon to men. What ordinary man could approach such a predator and live?"

"At first, I was afraid, and I felt I would be eaten. I grasped the stones tighter and concentrated on my breathing, trying to slow my heartbeat. With every step I felt my heart pounding slower, and slower still. When I neared the beast, I realized it was not my heart pounding, but his; and it was not fear he displayed, it was a show of strength."

Danaà delivered a firm slap upon Beedxe's shoulder. This he followed with a grunt and a nod of encouragement. They could tell stories around the fire later, but this was not the time. This was the time to prepare camp.

A common camping site for travelers spanning many generations, few preparations were needed. Stones had already been arranged in a large circle to contain their fire, and larger stones were placed a few feet back from those to be used as seats. As with most sites common to travelers, just a brief tidying of the area was necessary.

With a relatively small fire burning for warmth, the group gathered around its safety. While the light of a fire made the immediate surroundings easier to see and kept many animals at bay, a fire too large could attract the wrong kind of attention. This was the Oaxaca way of life—to fight for land, power, and to appease one's gods While there may have been safety in numbers, even greater safety lay in awareness and attentiveness.

The guards often chewed on roasted agave stalks while performing nighttime duties. The nectar sealed within the roasted stalks provided chewiness and sweetness which aided in keeping them alert. The guards remained stationary instead of roving as they may do while guarding a militant campsite.

Meanwhile, Danaà led stories in whispered speech. These tales were spoken into the flames that emanated from the fire. Flames that tickled ones' amusement while provoking the deepest pits of eager imagination.

Pleasantries out of the way, they planned for the next day's events before bedding down for the night. They lay in relative proximity to the fire and slumbered peacefully as the king's guard kept watch. They slipped into the world of dreams, into the realm of Pecala.

CHAPTER 3

DAWN IS RISING. *HE SEES THROUGH NARROWED EYES, HIS BREATHING still and steady, his heart pounding. Before him, he sees a northern tamandua: black vest upon yellow fur, the prehensile tail still wrapped around the tree it descends from. Ten pounds of anteater making his blood boil and mouth salivate with anticipation. Still now; watching as the unsuspecting tamandua lets loose of the tree with no regard for its own safety. It sinks its snout into an ant mound the size of a yucca plant.*

The unsuspecting meal goes frantically to gluttonous work, devouring the ants as they scurry about frantically. Around him, the forest goes still and quiet. Sharp, retractable claws stealthily raise muscular mass; slowly and deftly the predator maneuvers itself into a crouching stance. The smell of the tamandua fills the early morning air. The fur on the nape of his neck is rising as pulsing veins ache with hunger.

Beedxe' stirs in his sleep, realizing he is now one with the jaguar. He begins to embrace it, he yearns for it, he *is* the jaguar! Muscles fire with reckless abandon as he makes a mad dash, lunging at his prey. The ambush takes only a fraction of a moment, soundless and efficient. Canine teeth are his weapon of choice, and he delivers the killer bite through the skull of the tamandua. Jaguars, it seems, have an affinity for piercing the skull of their prey for the kill. Blood flows into his eager mouth as his unsuspecting prey turns limp and lifeless.

"Beedxe', wake up, wake up!" Ayotli is shaking him frantically, as it appears his young friend is entranced. "Are you ok? You were growling, grunting and, and, and … I don't know what you were doing! What were you doing?"

"Do you have a connection with the jaguar now?" Danaà asked. "First contact is physical, like yesterday. If first contact creates a bond, you may receive an invitation through dream or vision."

"Yes, uija-tào. We were hunting, killing, tasting blood for the first time. Tamandua, it seems, is a fine meal in these parts." Beedxe' appeared to be bragging; gloating with a menacing smile. That smile unnerved Ayotli who felt the chill of the morning cool streak up his spine. He shook it off with a shiver.

"Sounds repulsive, yuck! Speaking of breakfast, what are we having? Beedxe' may choose to have his raw, but I would prefer cooked."

"A fine breakfast, of course! Squash blossoms and nopales. Sorry Beedxe', no meat. You may continue to savor the taste of your kill while imagining the nopales are tamandua." Danaà teased, be it through a jealous mind. After all, fresh cactus pads and squash blossoms were not only a tasty start to the day, but they contained much needed hydration. They would need the hydration as they crossed the desert-like dryness of the valley floor.

As they slowly consumed their bountiful treats a song played overhead. Beedxe's attention was drawn to a pair of west Mexican chachalaca birds nestled high atop the cypress tree. The two birds heralded the morning and celebrated the sunrise with their signature cha-cha-laca hymns. Not overly imposing in size or stature, they boasted a long neck, a long tail, feathers of brown and grey, along with a red fleshy throat. A beautiful bird, which is brash in nature, the chachalaca sings beautifully unless perturbed, in which case they can be quite the nuisance.

"Do the birds make you hungry again Beedxe'?" Ayotli just can't let it go. The newly minted manhood of his young compadre had been accented by the ability to reside within the mind and spirit of the most revered predator in their world. "What did the beast taste like anyway?"

Letting out a whimsical giggle Beedxe' answered, "Warm, salty and, … I don't know, maybe a little like nibbling on a bone from uija-tào's famous soup."

"Ah, so my cooking wins the day! I always knew you liked that soup. Your mouth always said no, but your eyes said mm-mm yes!" Danaà let loose something between a snort and a chuckle, call it a snuckle.

"You must make sure we are served something worthy of your concoction when we get to Monte Albàn. Surely they will they serve us good food!" Beedxe' thought with his stomach first, as all young men do.

"When you witness the wonders of the great city, and kneel before its king and queen, you will be too preoccupied with awe to have such hunger. The king will inquire upon your abilities as a nagual. You must tell him very little. Do not lie, but do not fill his mind with ideas that only a nagual could understand. Does that sound like something you can do?

"Yes Danaà, I will tell him I have made a connection and that I am still growing into my skin ... well, fur. Does that sound acceptable?"

"Cool, cunning, and crafty, much like the spirit of the beast. I like it. Well, I suppose we should be on our way. We must stop to harvest the seeds of the moonflower." With a wave and a gesture, the great seer motions his guard detail to lead the way.

"I still do not understand why the guards must remain anonymous to us. I have much jewelry to barter at the great event, nothing like an early start." Ayotli, ever the businessman, was looking to re-hone his bartering skills. While commoners were permitted to wear simple forms of jewelry, they were disallowed precious metals and stones. Common jewelry, like that worn by Ayotli, comprised mostly of well carved ubiquitous stones; it was often held together by twine or plain metals.

"It is not anonymity my little friend, you and I are the bridge between the guards and the nagual. Beedxe' must be protected from everyone, including himself." Looking at Beedxe', Danaà slowly nods his head in a manner commanding the young nagual to nod back in agreement. Beedxe' nods with fierce enthusiasm. Even his eyes have been remade; they boy is truly changed. His face has lost its childlike jubilance along with much of its innocence. Danaà sees years of discipline and purpose that have remarkably manifested themselves overnight, no doubt caused by the hunt.

"I see now." Ayotli seems saddened by the fact that his coy, silly friend has lost his youthful exuberance. Perhaps a joke to see if he still has it. "Given a choice between the white-nosed coati, the rabbit, and the tamandua; which would make the finer meal my friend?"

A raspy throated snicker has replaced the boys charming giggle. "I think I would prefer to hunt the rabbit, just for the chase. The coali would be a good meal, perhaps a little fatty. But I never got past the blood taste of the tamandua, so I guess that would be my choice for now. I have this unfulfilled hunger to taste its flesh." He paused as he saw the nervous smile on the little man's face. "I still prefer my meat cooked, served with chilis and tetechas. Relax, my friend."

"Tetechas are bound to be plentiful as we move further into the valley. Perhaps we should gather some along with the moonflower seed pods, and top that off with biznaga for our queen." Danaà, now, was thinking with his belly.

"Oh, I love biznaga! Should we gather enough, we could nibble on some to cap off a perfect journey. Surely Beedxe' has not lost his taste for cactus candy," Ayotli quickly answered.

"I have only ever had what was brought to me from the two of you, various visitors and my parents. Are they even sweeter when the plump cacti are freshly plucked? Uija-tào, will there be time to prepare the treat?"

"Of course! We cannot take an unprepared offering to our beautiful queen. Upon beginning our harvest, we will send the soldiers home to the mountain; we will have no further use for them. Now, how about a little silence? You're making me hungry and I just ate." A playful yet stern smile parked itself on his face.

They exited the shade canopy of the pine forest, crossing into the unforgiving dryness of the rocky terrain. There seemed to be no transition, just a clean-cut line separating trees from brush. Perhaps the cypress was planted by the gods. With the silence commanded upon them by Danaà their senses were free to wonder. Morning rays from the newly risen sun were upon them, dancing as if flames on a fire.

The river they have been following now trickled down to a brook or a stream. "This is where we shake loose our escort; we no longer require their presence." Danaà stated as he turned his attention to the guards. "Thank you, my friends! Safe journey to you. We will be along."

The detail abruptly turned and waved, then just as abruptly, re-established their course and marched on. Danaà was not just a priest of elite bloodlines, but he was uija-tào (the great seer). Through status and title, he commanded respect and projected strength and confidence. The guards would follow any commands given.

"We cross here where the waters are shallow. The tall patch of brush protruding from amongst the cacti is the moonflower. Can you smell them from here Beedxe'?"

"Yes, uija-tào. It is a very pungent aroma. Is it a pleasing a odor to the gods? Surely the smell is not the appeal!"

"It is not the smell which the gods find irresistible, but the beauty of the star shaped flowers. Not to mention, these precious plants possess the strength to grow rapidly in this harsh and dry climate. The smell, young one, is much more intense during hours of darkness."

They hastened their pace in anticipation of the divinity the moonflower holds. As they drew closer, the odor invaded their senses. Known to cause sickness and hallucinations when handled improperly, the aroma reminded them to take precautions before handling the vines.

A large green iguana perched upon an even larger boulder a few feet away from the moonflower stems. The smaller dorsal spines running along the length of the back showed it to be a female. She sat drenched in sunshine, captured by its essence from which she would draw strength. Her eyes were closed as she appeared to be sleeping. She sat still, relying on her parietal eye to sense danger and movement. The ocelot, however, carried too much stealth for the use of a mere parietal eye.

Creeping behind the natural cover afforded it from moon-flower vines, the ocelot moved undetected. The three men halt their advance towards the plant, anticipating the show that was about to commence. With a white chest and yellow back, the ocelot is adorned with a maze of spotted black lines. Its eyes are engulfed by the deepest hazel surrounded by pits as dark as tar. A dwarf when compared to the size of a jaguar, but it never lacks in skill or cunning. It stopped, as still as the rocks surrounding it, savoring the kill to come. Ambush! The incursion contained a ravaging onslaught of violence that ceased within seconds. Not a drop of blood was visible as the stealthy cat glanced at its audience as if for applause, then exited the area with its lifeless and motionless dinner.

"Well", Ayotli starts nearly breathless, "How does that rate with the skill of the beast you spirited Beedxe'? I mean, it was just an iguana, but that was a feisty and ravenous display."

"That was amazing! No sound, no struggle, no problem! Iguana is a fine meal and I am sure master ocelot will fill his belly. I have to admit a little jealousy, seems like weeks since we had iguana. Huh uija-tào?"

"Trying to make us hungry again Beedxe'? If we see another, perhaps we will prepare it with the biznaga! Now, you two harvest those two fat biznaga cacti and I will gather the seeds from the moonflower. Promise me you will not cut the moonflower until I have trained you properly Beedxe'. Predators are not the only things that kill out here."

"I won't, but is this not a good time to train me? We are here at the very site after all," Beedxe' countered.

"Perhaps after the offerings and blessings are complete and we are on our way back to Lyobaa. It may seem trivial, but even priests of my status must follow protocol. The gods dictate, remember this." Danaà straightens his fingers and points to the sky with his entire hand extended.

"Yes, uija-tào."

With that, the three go to work. Hands, eyes, and minds must work together while cultivating a cactus. Instead of trying to watch the high priest work, the pair work together to cut and pluck the needles from the cacti one at a time. Peeling and slicing the desert treat was quick and easy with sharper-than-steel obsidian blades.

Putting the slices into some spare sacks Ayotli had tucked away in his pack, they could not help but to sample some of the smaller chunks that conveniently separated themselves from the supply they as they packed. Beedxe' used his water flask and rinsed off a flattened rock to use as a platter. It was as if the gods themselves had made a platter accessible for their use.

"Are you done over there, uija-tào?" Beedxe' was ready to eat! "It is so juicy and sweet! Best not to let it bake in the sun."

Danaà was too busy obsessing over his work. Every part of the godly moonflower was capable of causing visions. These visions were not meant to be seen outside of ceremonial traditions. One could lose his or her mind by following false visions which were not provided by the gods.

Danaà wore gloves usually used by those who would play the ceremonial ball game of the known world. He plucked the seed pods, which were clearly splitting open and ready to spill their divine cargo. The spiny seedling pods have the size and shape of a chachalaca egg. They split into four equal chambers when ready for propagation. Carefully placing the seeds into a small purse-like bag, Danaà was almost ready to rejoin the hungry pair.

"Allow me a moment to clean my hands in the river. You need not wait on me, but do not eat my share." He looked at the pair raising an eyebrow in a playful manner. "I will need nourishment as well. Not to mention I can almost taste the sweet flesh of the biznaga already!"

Walking back to the low stream-like area of the river, Danaà savored the sweetness of this delicatessen to come. He must still have his wits about him, protection from the gods did not always include protection from the rattling serpents which adorned the floor of the valley. Kneeling by the river and briskly rubbing his hands, Danaà was audience to a group of vermillion flycatcher birds singing and bathing in the same waters not less than a rock throw away. The red and brown birds were vibrant in color, the vessels that contained their spirits were rivaled only by their pleasing song.

Standing and wiping his hands on his garb, he turned back to his travel companions. "It is a perfect day, the birds sing, the ocelot feeds and we will honor our king and queen before the gods. From the clear arid skies, the lightning of Cocijo will present itself!" Danaà spoke as if he knew the minds of the gods; but then again, he was the great seer. Did he not foretell the coming of the nagual?

The three sat together now. They would smile if they we not so busy inhaling their meal. Sweet, juicy biznaga formed rivers of nectar, which flowed from their chins. The trio washed it down with water, knowing they would need nourishment and hydration for the walk up to the hill-top capital of their empire.

• • •

"LET'S TAKE A FEW MOMENTS IN SELF-REFLECTION FOR REST. MONTE Albàn calls to us, but we must be ready for her grandeur. There will be games, prayers, offerings and the needs of the people must be tended to. Remember, Beedxe', you are a priest of the gods and for the people." Danaà said, instructing his pupil in protocol. "We do not decide who is sick, who will live or who will die. We watch for signs from the gods, but the gods do not hear the prayers of men; that is what our ancestors are for."

"But, uija-tào, you are descended from the cloud people, my people are descended from the earth. The cloud people's prayers are answered by the gods. You pray to your ancestors so that they may speak for you … what about Ayotli and I?"

Though still a young priests apprentice, Beedxe' knew Zapotec traditions stated that only the elites in society were descended from the gods. Zapotec, common and elite, prayed to their ancestors, not to the gods.

"Try not to think of it as those who have proceeded us. We all pray to our ancestors. Some ancestors are from the earth and others are from the clouds, this only reflects origins and destinations; it is merely a path our spirits must follow. I know others would say only those descended from the cloud people may speak through their ancestors to the gods, but I have seen differently. One day a new truth may be revealed, leaving us with one clear conclusion. I am the great seer; am I not?"

"You are a father to us all, uija-tào. When my mother and father passed into the underworld you were all I had. Until now, I honestly thought you were just grooming me to be a nagual. I now know you to be a father."

"And you are a son to me Beedxe'. Yes, I was grooming you to be a nagual. I was also grooming a man and, should the gods agree, a replacement when I grow too old. As the great seer, I see the will of the gods. I see omens and translate those omens to what is to come. Should the gods see fit to make you the great seer, you would see so much more. You would see the heart and desire of the jaguar, you would be one with the most ferocious of the gods' beasts. This, and everything which is to come, is in the hands of the gods."

"I will do all that is required of me. Tonight, I shall pray to my parents. I have not done so in a few days; my mother will be proud to hear of my communion with nature."

Danaà turned now to his other companion. "And your prayers Ayotli? Have you honored your ancestors?"

"I think of them every day. My grandfather seems to be the only one which I can depend on to guide me. Is this uncommon?" Ayotli had never mentioned this before; but many questions often go unasked.

"The spirits of the dead choose when to speak. Do not think of it in terms of good and bad, or even as right and wrong. We cannot truly know until we have joined them in the afterlife. Perhaps one day others will answer your prayers. If not, my little friend, that is their loss." A manly slap on the back from Danaà straightened the posture of Ayotli. Pride was in posture and we should stand as tall as we can manage.

"Come now!" Barked Danaà, pointing towards their destination. "Atop that mountain is the great city! One day it will have stunning walls and be a heavily fortified and impregnable fortress; truly worthy of godly protection."

"Does its elevation really make it closer to the gods?" Inquired Beedxe'. "Are the rumors true that you can hear them? Feel them?"

"When your apprenticeship is complete, you will feel them. You have seen through the eyes and the spirit of the jaguar; your transformation will mark another milestone in your young life. All things in time, and time has almost come." Danaà smiled menacingly and shrugged his shoulders.

The march began anew, and Beedxe' still had more questions than answers. They had been able to see the great city for some time now, but from afar it appeared to be like any other mountain top. From a distance, it appeared to be naught but rock. The man-chiseled flat top of the mountain was now more pronounced due to their close proximity. Pyramids, straight lines of structures, and even smoke from the fires could be clearly seen.

Still viewing the city from the valley floor and approaching from the southeast, the palace complex was in view along with a clear line of sight to the heaven shaped observatory. Slow, long nights spent watching and studying celestial bodies would be accentuated by inhabiting this building which resembled those stars.

"You see! All structures are built and oriented from north to south save one, the observatory. While the observatory is on line with the structures in the center, it is not built in a north-south manner. The building is shaped to mimic the constellation of light.

Coquihani, god of light, inhabits the brightest star within this celestial body. When the sun rises tomorrow, Coquihani will rise with it. The power of the two rising together will allow for your transformation."

A horrified look raced it way upon the face of Beedxe', mortifying him with fear. It was one thing for a nagual to see through the eyes of his spirit animal, but transformation, well, that's a whole different ball of wax.

"Do not look so worried, young one. You must embrace the light and the change. I am not nagual, I cannot tell you how it feels. I can tell you, however, that I have foreseen your shapeshifting prowess. You must be confident! You must show the people and the gods alike that you are nagual! Can you do this?"

"Will the tonic give me bravery? Will it calm me?" Beedxe' asked frantically searching for strength.

"The tonic will give you vision. The tonic will open your eyes and allow you communion with your jaguar spirit. You will not inhabit the senses of a jaguar as you did before, you will become a jaguar. You will run faster than you ever have. You will hunt with stealth and power. And then, when the gods are pleased, the lightning of Cocijo will draw you home and calm your vexation."

Now feeling re-centered with some hunger and humor coming back, Beedxe' said, "And you will make me my soup?" He couldn't shake the taste of that soup.

"Of course! Your passage to manhood will be complete and you may eat what you like. Let's wait until then to see what you hunger for, Beedxe'." As they finally approached the base of the mountain Danaà drew a breath. "So, we have a short jaunt up the side of this mountain, and the walking part of our journey is complete. Ready?"

"I am ready to honor you and the gods, uija-tào. I am ready to prove to our king, to our queen, and to everyone that I am a nagual; but, before we ascend to the top of the mountain, pay me one favor, please."

"If it is within my power, of course I will," Danaà said. Looking at the sprightly expression which manifested itself across the boy's mischievous and nefarious face.

Beedxe' raised an eyebrow, a smile slowly grew upon his face. He cast a glance at their small travel companion. "Tell Ayotli there is a rattling serpent near his foot."

"Aieeeee!" Ayotli screamed, jumped, then paced frantically trying to recompose himself.

Beedxe' and Danaà enjoyed the amusing display Ayotli performed for them. The small, unassuming man slowly made his way behind them, keeping his eyes peeled on the pygmy rattlesnake now coiling just a few feet away.

"This new sense of humor has becoming alarming my friend. That serpent could have killed me!" Ayotli muttered while composing himself.

"Relax," Beedxe' said, "They say the serpents are just as scared of us as we are of them. Clearly, you have frightened the little snake."

Still not looking amused, Ayotli said with a sneer, "Then why did I not hear him screaming?"

All of them, even Ayotli now, were laughing, but the snake brought them back to the reality of the Oaxaca; dangers lie in every step! Then, with all of the pleasantries out of the way, up the hill they went.

CHAPTER 4

Poor little Ayotli was gasping for breath and bracing himself with his newly acquired walking stick as they crested the top of the hill. He looked as if his lungs were bursting. His once rosy cheeks were now blood red, his eyes filled with the resolve required to get the job done.

The city opened itself as if inviting weary travelers into the sacred breast of the mountain. The long straight lines Beedxe' noticed while standing on the valley floor now stretched endlessly, as far as his eyes could see. Unlike the fretted walls that adorned Lyobaa, these walls were made of rock and mortar. Obviously, the walls were pieced together from bits of rock jarred loose from the mountain top.

"All right there, Ayotli?" Danaà seemed a little out of breath himself. "What a pleasant walk, aye Beedxe'?"

"That was great! We should go to the bottom and do it again!" Knowing he too could use a bit of a breather. "Maybe Ayotli would like to rest for a moment."

Ayotli giggled through shortened breath, "I am just getting started! There is much to do, many items I wish to barter for. Not to mention, I hope our beautiful queen will fall in love with the gifts I made for her!"

"I certainly hope you have them ready. I'll direct the sentries to take us to the palace immediately. The king will no doubt be excited about the coming rituals and, of course, the arrival of Beedxe'." Being uija-tào was more than just a position of honor. Danaà must have his wits about him and interpret the signs of the gods correctly.

No sooner had Danaà announced his intentions than a sentry from the palace complex approached them. Danaà was the spiritual leader of the Zapotec empire, and the sentry would be expected to extend him every courtesy. Not recognizing the great seer would be an embarrassment.

The sentry was everything one would expect. He was of an average height, but well built. One could tell by watching his movements, he knew how to handle himself. His face was decorated with a large battle scar that seemed to make a crater from his forehead, around his brow and down the back of his ear. *Amazing*, Beedxe' thought, *to have such an injury and still be in possession of that ear.*

"Uija-tào! Welcome! We have been awaiting your arrival. The king is anxious to see you, but I think the queen waits for jewelry from Ayotli." He smiled and nodded at Ayotli. Ayotli returned the nod with his own smile of excitement. Obviously, the two man were already well acquainted with one another.

"I have been possessed by one spirit and then the next. Even I am in disbelief of my own craftsmanship. Perhaps you would be interested in some of the common jewelry I have crafted?" Making jewelry for common citizens was much simpler than crafting fine gems and precious metals for the elites. The obvious difference to Ayotli was that elite jewelry was given to elites to garner favor;

common jewelry, however, was something he could use to barter for goods from other merchants.

"We will see, my friend. And this must be the young apprentice we have heard so much about. There has not been a nagual in my life time, I look forward to your passage into manhood and into beast."

Beedxe' tilted his head in a thankful manner in appreciation of his acceptance.

"I am Kabil. I will take you now, to the king." The sentry gestured at his coming replacement and motioned him to keep an eye out. "Come, please, the king demanded to be informed the minute you arrived, uija-tào."

They made their way through a fairly wide passage way until the entire city seemed to peel open like a giant ear of corn. Not even remotely similar to their meager accommodations in Lyobaa, the city was alive with mega structures. Immediately in front of them, Beedxe' noticed the observatory begging for attention. Large conquest slabs with images of vanquished opponents are separated by a thick mortar. The tormented souls depicted on them are often carved into the stone with their heads detached and the names of the fallen cities also listed on the trophies.

"A testament to the greatness of our kings! Many of the vanquished cities choose to surrender and join us without bloodshed. Conquest is gratifying, but to peacefully negotiate integration and conformity, that's an art form. Diplomacy is a very useful tool when dealing with peoples who are willing to submit to the true gods. Mercy can often define greatness more aptly than conquest, understand?" Danaà asked Beedxe'.

With eyes now bulging out of his head, Beedxe' nodded silently, still awe-struck. Danaà grabbed firm hold of the shoulders of his young priest and turned him to face the wide-open plaza. As promised, the buildings ran in north-south lines ... on line! It was both puzzling and inspiring how men could make such long, straight lines of structures.

Offerings of fruits, meats and maize were abundantly stacked on a stairway to his right. As his eyes traveled up the stairway, they were filled with the vision of a couple dressed in vibrant clothing. The king and queen waited patiently for the arrival of the great seer and of the nagual. Adorned in fashions made from the finest cotton in the region. The queen's garb consisted of the deepest, darkest blue; accented with a yellow color worthy of the shiniest gold. The king wore a light green shaded with black undertones. Their piercings and necklaces shone with the brightest gold, silver, emerald and jade.

Danaà and Beedxe' ascended the stairway, leaving Ayotli kneeling at the base of the steps. "Keep your calm Beedxe', priests must always project calm."

"Yes, uija-tào. I am frozen by their greatness but calmed by your tone. Thank you for your teachings." Beedxe' spoke under his breath so none but his mentor could hear him.

"Uija-tào! I was worried you may have gotten lost! The ceremonies will begin in mere hours. Where have you been?" King Kasakir smiled and gave a bravado laden laugh. "My guards left you at daybreak."

"Great king," Danaà and Beedxe' knelt before them. "We had to persuade the moonflower to bless us with the gods' bounty. This night will be a night to remember for generations to come." As the two were gestured to stand, Danaà firmly planted the side of his fist on the shoulder of Beedxe'. "I am pleased to introduce you to my pupil and our nagual. Beedxe', has already bonded with the spirit jaguar on our journey. He is ready."

"Yes," said the king, "the guards told of a beast calmed by a mere boy. They told me of a boy becoming a man in moments, they told me of calm and bravery before a hungry predator, they told me of inner power." He turned to look at Beedxe'. "I trust the journey was a pleasant one."

"Yes, great king. This was my first time outside the walls of Lyobaa. I felt like a caged animal being released." Beedxe' spoke humbly.

"And you still believe his shapeshifting gift can be accomplished through rite and ritual Danaà?" The king was quick to confirm.

"As the sun and Coquihani rise, my king. Blessings will shower upon us as the two rise in unison."

Queen Zyanya joined the conversation now. "All glory to the gods, this will truly be a celebration to remember. To have a new king willingly submitting to our kingdom at sunset tonight, and then a nagual at sunrise, pure divinity will descend upon us. But, is that Ayotli I see kneeling below us?" The queen was ready to be showered with gifts of beauty before being showered with the blessings of the divine. "Join us, Ayotli."

Ayotli moved quickly up the stairs while remaining partially hunched over in a display of obedience. "My queen, I have brought you a necklace and a bracelet of pure jade. I have worked feverishly for many hours shaping and polishing these works of art. Of course, they are mere stones compared to your beauty." Few men had the skill and patience Ayotli possessed. The ability to create such ornate designs from precious stones was his specialty. Others smelted silver or gold expertly to which Ayotli had some skill; but gemstones, the very best designs were dominated by Ayotli.

"Quickly then!" She said with the excitement and exuberance of a child. "Let's see them."

Ayotli removed a deer pelt from his bag. Wrapped with the softest part of fur towards the jewels. He unfolded it slowly, displaying his unique expertise when it came to presentation. "It is my honor to present you with my most ornate works of art yet. The beads and amulet, made of pure jade, my queen; the designs you see in the beads are that of the clouds. The three loops are the centerpiece of the necklace, they represent wisdom, beauty and perfection. All together they are meant to appease Pecala, god of dreams; may he bring you only the most pleasant of dreams, my queen." Ever the salesman, he poured his soul into the tribute.

Queen Zyanya, with eyes the size of the coming moon, inspected the items with joy and fervor. As she looked closely, she could see the fine lines of the clouds etched into each bead of the bracelet and necklace. Upon close inspection of the loops, she noticed they were polished to a mind-numbing brightness. "How do you get them so shiny?" Conversation, not really a question.

"I believe Pecala himself guided my hands. Not for me, my queen, for you. Something, a spirit perhaps, seemed to consume me as I worked. I have never felt this before, surely these are my finest creations!" Still the salesman, ever the showman.

"Ayotli," King Kasakir interjected, "I thank you for your gifts to the queen, they will not go unrewarded. Now, run along with Kabil." Looking to the sentry now, "Kabil, take the queen's jeweler to fill his belly."

"Uija-tào!" Ayotli pointed at the other bag containing the sweet biznaga cactus for the king and queen.

"Ah, I almost forgot! Beedxe' and Ayotli prepared a treat for you while I was plucking the moonflower" Danaà motioned his ecstatic friend to present the sweet nourishment to the kingdom's divine couple.

"You and your companions spoil us uija-tào. You should come more often." The King Kasakir said with a smile and a fist placed firmly against the heart of Danaà. "Bring the young nagual into the palace, I have many questions."

Of course, my king. May I request that you keep it brief? There are still preparations to be made and it has been a very eventful time for my young pupil. Best not to sway his thoughts too far from his current meditations." Zapotec priests, especially the great seer, were treated with high regard; even the most elite of society, including royalty, dared not interfere with godly matters.

"Just enough to satisfy my curiosity, you understand." Respecting the wishes of his priests were not always easy for the leader of the known world. "Begin your preparations then. I will have a brief, private word; then he will be along. Surely the gods would look favorably towards a king conversing with the young nagual?"

"As you command, my king." A paternal nod to Beedxe', and he was on his way.

The king led Beedxe' toward a shaded area located in the front partition of the palace. "Come, have a seat young one. No need to be nervous." Beedxe' cautiously moved under the ceiling of the palace and plopped himself down with all of the courtesy he could muster. "Now, tell me what goes on in the mind of the beast?"

"My spirit jaguar and I made contact in dream but one time, divine one, there is not much to tell. I was asleep, then entranced. I could see, hear and feel everything that the beast could. He was gracious enough to allow me the pleasure of a hunt, then I woke."

"So! A hunt! How glorious! May I ask what the kill was, young one? Surely the hunt was not without meaning." King Kasakir was visibly excited now, his eyes observed Beedxe' with fierce curiosity.

"Tamandua, my king. He … we, pierced the skull of the tamandua rendering it lifeless. I can still remember the taste of its blood. But, as I told you, I was awakened immediately upon the taste of blood."

"The cunning and crafty cat showed you what he wanted you to see. That is the way it works with the nagual. My father told me of the ways of the nagual when I was a child. During the early years of my father's rule they had a nagual. He died an old man, celebrated by the people. On his death bed he told my father what I share with you now. The beast shares only with he whom he trusts … you!" A firm pat on his right knee from the king's palm. "Now, off you go, prepare for your spectacle."

Beedxe' stood tall, bowed and waited for a permissive wave. The wave was granted in an elegant manner, and off he went. The young man moved purposefully but not hurriedly from beneath the shade of the palace, then down the steps. Awaiting him and barking instructions to his fellow priests, Danaà gestured him over.

"All went well?" An inquisitive look matched his tone.

"Yes, Yes, of course. But you did not tell me the father of the king knew a nagual. The great one shared this with me."

"He never told me of such." Danaà seemed puzzled the king kept this from him. "I guess now I can understand why he has always inquired upon you and demanded your protection. Did he seem pleased?"

"Yes, uija-tào. He told me that I was shown only what the beast wanted me to see. He also said the beast showed me because of trust … a bond."

"He is wise as he is powerful, and he is also correct. Come, we are almost ready."

The final preparations needed to be made for the upcoming spectacle. Wood must be stacked for fire, torches must be readied, and the priests must have time to prepare. There were many cities under the rule of the Zapotec, each with its own priest. These priests drew strength and wisdom form their spiritual leader, their uija-tào.

Once everything was in order and offerings were placed near the altar for the gods, the priests would have a short time to decompress and meditate before changing into traditional clothing more suited for the pageantry of ceremonial prayers.

• • •

DUSK WAS SETTING IN THE OAXACA. THE PRIESTS GATHERED IN front of the palace now, often times in such big events there may be twenty or more, and tonight was no exception. Each was dressed in his traditional white robe and white headdress. Colorful feathers and semi-precious stones adorned the headdress, crafted from materials from the priests' lineage. One priest stood out, uija-tào; the high priest and great seer. Over his white robe he wore a long vest of orange and black with images of sacred animals upon it. The jaguar, ocelot, wolf, and fox among other species adorned the great vest. Visible from a distance was the gleaming necklace Ayotli fashioned for him.

The great uija-tào spoke now. He called Beedxe' forward; but why? The transformation was to be at daybreak and that was many hours away. "We have traditions that must be honored before we continue with the night's offering." He said to Beedxe'.

Looking now to the crowd and more so to the elites, Danaà raised his voice to trumpet his proclamation to the crowd. "Beedxe', my pupil, lost his mother and father when he was just a child. I have, myself, raised this youngling in our ways. I have looked after this child and watched him become a man, never telling him that which may unduly swell his confidence." There's that menacing smile on Danaà's face again.

"Beedxe', as your father was my brother, you are my blood. In truth nephew, you are descended from Cocijo. Not just a nagual, but a nagual of the gods and sent to us from the gods." There was no shock from the crowd. Beedxe', it seems, was the last to know. "You do not think one would be entrusted with the will of the gods through mere coincidence, do you? I cannot help to notice, however, that you are that last among us to be presented his proper headdress. Ayotli …"

Another surprise the old jeweler kept from him with success! The headdress was simple and white with one gem only. An ornately carved and polished onyx, this could only be the work of Ayotli. The boy remained silent as the headdress was passed from Ayotli to Danaà and then, as if centuries had passed in mere minutes, it found its perch atop the head of Beedxe'.

Chants and blessings filled the air and shook the very foundations of the mountain. There, beside the fire laden altar, Beedxe' had finally arrived. His stance felt taller, his shoulders felt as if their strength could carry the burdens of his people and his mind grew silent in self-contemplation.

"Tonight, we honor Cocijo! We make these offerings in hopes of rain and a fruitful harvest to feed the people of our kingdom!" A priest Beedxe' had never seen before accompanied Danaà. He carried with him a lighted torch, a bundle of feathers and a bundle of agave needles. "Beedxe', your blood is pure and unstained. You will be first, and you will no longer be my pupil; from this night you are the pupil of the heavens and of the gods."

Priests took blood for offerings made to the gods from many places; among them the ears, nose, tongue, and genitals. He had come to think this part would be easy. Beedxe' grabbed the stabbing instrument with his right hand and quickly, so as to avoid the very thought of pain, thrust it into his left earlobe. As so many young priests do their first time, Beedxe' struck too hard and wide and the bright red blood let out. Blood, as thick as swamp waters found in the mangroves, oozed with purpose. Quickly the second priest handed Beedxe' a single feather which Beedxe' saturated with his own blood. He proudly thrust his fist, clenching the feather, into the air. Awaiting confirmation from the crowd's roar, he then cast the feather into the fire. There was a brief crackle from the fire and the burning stench that followed. As the stench subsided there was a brief rumble in the clear skies above.

Uija-tào and his second now moved from priest to priest. Each priest made his offering of blood to Cocijo, and each summoned a a rumble from the still and cloudless skies. Each priest seemed to allow the spirits to guide their piercing instrument to a suitable portion of their anatomy, the sweet spot that would draw the approval of Cocijo himself. The final priest to offer tribute was Danaà. Piercing the needle through the fatty tissue of the right nostril, the great uija-tào thrust the needle briskly now, ejecting the needle and bloodflow spewing from the opposite side.

Tossing the blood laden feather into the flames of the altar, Danaà turned to stoke the fires of the crowd. The bloodlust fueled chants from the crowd seemed to enrage the fire, its flames angrily reaching to the skies. Danaà turned his attention now to the surrendering king.

Remembering the lessons of diplomacy taught to him earlier in the day, Beedxe' could now make sense of why a king would surrender his village to the more powerful king of the Zapotec, King Kasakir. Better to save one's people than to die a fool.

"King Ikal, leader of the newly born Zapotec peoples to the north, do you offer the strength of your people to King Kasakir? And do you offer your blood and spirit, and the spirits of your people to the great Cocijo, god of lightning and rain?" Danaà's voice carried like the howl of the grey wolf. King Kasakir and his queen bowed their heads, receiving the gift of kinship from the surrendering king.

"I thank the great King Kasakir for his wisdom, mercy and leadership. I make tribute to the lightning god as proof of my submission and loyalty." Humbled, yet strong in resolve, King Ikal took a single knee beside the altar. He would renounce his title as king, but all citizens from elite bloodlines would keep their status as descendants of the gods. He would remain the ranking elite of his village, but answer to the true king, the Zapotec king, to King Kasakir.

Danaà, upon a ritualistic wave from King Kasakir, handed a chiseled obsidian blade to the capitulating nobleman. The blade was shaped and polished into the image of a hummingbird beak, though a bit longer and adorned with a ceremonial bone hilt. Ikal had been administered the moonflower tonic mere minutes before the start of the ceremony. His pupils were dilated, and his breathing controlled; but the spirits would not guide his hand, he must submit blood from the flesh of his genital region.

Nobleman Ikal now looked for permission from his king. King Kasakir motioned wildly to the skies, proclaiming his acceptance of the conquered king as a Zapotec elite citizen. Slowly, purposely, the king turned and nodded to Ikal.

Without hesitation, Ikal raised his pleat, then thrust the blade through his penis. Growling and grunting in pain; defiance, not weakness, was displayed in his facial expressions. Soaking the feather to appease the lightning god he grimaced before tossing the blood-soaked feather into the fire.

Lightning crackled and filled the night sky as priests, elites and common citizens fell to their knees. Snapping, clamoring and appearing to spread throughout the now clouded sky, the storm was all around them. The valley was being drenched by torrential downpours while their great city remained dry. The entire city was once again on their feet, witnessing the power and greatness of the lightning god. Lightning continued to dominate the city sky while rain flooded the valley below.

"Blessings are bestowed on our lands by Cocijo in all of his divinity. In the name of our king, praise the gods ... fear the gods; Cocijo has arrived!" The great uija-tào now ignited the crowd with the same ferocity as the bolted lightning above. King Kasakir and

Queen Zyanya stood side by side, hands meeting between them. The lightning seemed to surround them as they raised their joined hands to the sky, embracing the approval of Cocijo. As the storm swelled around the city the excitement grew over promises of a lush and bountiful harvest, a harvest created by the lightning god for his loyal servants.

CHAPTER 5

FOLLOWING THE SPECTACLE, A GREAT CELEBRATION ERUPTED within the city. The hours of darkness were a perfect time to study the stars. A conglomeration of priests would normally gather for the celestial studies, but this night was all about the enlightenment of Beedxe'. Danaà called for his pupil. "Beedxe', not yet tired, are you?"

"No, uija-tào. Excitement still runs through me like the blood through the jaguar's heart. I have rested and studied my entire life. I do not believe I could sleep if I wanted to." The young priest no longer spoke as a child, Danaà could hardly believe how drastically the past two days had altered the thinking and speech patterns of the boy. How quickly he had become a man.

"We have a few hours to prepare for your true calling. I have sent the other priests to make preparations while you and I look to the heavens. Come, it is time to see the stars from the building fashioned to represent them." The observatory atop Monte Albàn was constructed to resemble the constellation of light, in future years it would come to be known as the constellation Auriga.

They approached from the northeast stairwell of the observatory, up the steps, and into a small corridor, then entered the observation room (clearly not made for more than two to three men). "Take a

51

small sip of this tonic Beedxe', the moonflower's gift from the gods. Relax your eyes, and just let the sky consume you. The heavens will soon appear brighter and come to life!" Danaà said.

The tropane alkaloids from the moonflower would take a few minutes to run their course, further dilating the pupils and allowing for intensification of vision during hours of darkness. Many have wondered how the ancients of Mesoamerica viewed celestial bodies, questioning the manner of study which would allow them to see objects that were so very distant in the night sky. Moonflower, the obvious answer, may have truly been a gift from the gods to allow mortals to view the realm of the gods. Care was taken to consume this tonic during hours of darkness as direct light could cause pain to enlarged pupils.

"Will I see the approaching Coquihani, uija-tào?" After witnessing the greatness of Cocijo, Beedxe' was ready for more visions of divinity.

"The light god Coquihani rises at dawn with the sun, so though we know this happens, we cannot see him. Remember, what we have seen of Cocijo was the strength of Cocijo, not the lightning god himself. With Coquihani's blessing, you will be confirmed as nagual. Some nagual are only blessed with visions from the eyes of the beasts they inhabit. I see in you the ability to transform and become the beast, this is very rare Beedxe'."

"I have been feeling restless." The newly confirmed man and priest confided in Danaà. "Where I once felt amused by the world, I now feel enraged by containment within it; I feel an itch for violence, uija-tào."

"The tonic and vastness of the heavens will help to contain that for a while, but the animal within you must have his say. Do not let it frighten you. Instead, accept that it is a part of you. You must control the beast until the rising of Coquihani has unleashed it." Uija-tào was wise, and the cupped palm placed on Beedxe's shoulder was reassuring.

Beedxe' could feel the tonic kicking him like a mule. His muscles stiffened, he could hear his own breathing; entranced, yet awake. A queasiness to the stomach set in briefly, but quickly dissipated. The stars came alive as if dancing in the sky. The beloved ancestors moved amongst the now brightly lit night sky. "I can see them! They move as if they are one with the wind!"

"You see Beedxe', you have visions only priests may possess. You must show caution and intellect, there are tricksters amongst the spirits. Breathe deeply in and out, trust your impulses more than your thoughts. In time you will learn to read the will of the gods from the spirits. Our ancestors occupy the stronghold between mortal men and the gods. Do you understand?"

"Yes, uija-tào, but the spirits are so distant. How do you know who they are, or if they are tricksters?"

"Try not to think of the person inhabiting the spirit, think of the intentions of the spirit instead. You will only know whom a spirit is during prayers with your ancestors. This is not prayer, this is observation and interpretation." Danaà's wisdom had led many young priests to see the will of the gods. The will of the gods was not always an easy path to follow, but gods, spirits and men must all do their parts. Obeying the false prophecies provided by any of these tricksters could have dire consequences.

The two priests stood together now. Master and pupil admired and observed the heavens. The spirits, it seemed, honored the prophecy as read by Danaà; a prophecy of a great nagual. The spirits moved, swayed and portrayed themselves as beasts. One after another seemed to transform themselves. So many animals were portrayed! Along with the jaguar, there were wolves, birds and even donkeys.

"They show many animals, uija-tào. Are these spirits of the nagual? Do the nagual speak to me now?" Beedxe' asked.

"Perhaps. Some of them may have been nagual. They are simply here to honor your transformation, into and out of the body of a jaguar. Some nagual never return to the bodies of men, they are truly beasts trapped within men. It appears as though you will return to us upright, as a man." The great priest was an expert in evaluating communications made by spirits.

"I guess I never thought about whether I would come back or not." Beedxe' stated, nervously laughing. "That's good to know! While I enjoyed the hunt, I also enjoy walking upright." The two shared a comedic moment beneath the spirits as Beedxe' playfully acted out transforming from beast back to man. "Yes, standing upright is a good thing!"

"Come, Beedxe', let's have some water and enjoy the night air. I'm parched and you, well, you will need the water as well. Your journey, no doubt, will require a good bit of exercise"

A wink and a nod carried the two back through the corridor and into the whispering breeze of the night air. The city, not quiet nor filled with sleepy eyes, was still awake and attentive. Hushed conversations collided with the stoking and crackling of fires. Wolves howled, and bats flew overhead as if awaiting the spectacle to come. People began to shuffle through the plaza, greeting one another with word and gesture. Something was about to happen, something grand and filled with divinity sent from the light god

himself. Wind carried word, word carried rumor, but none knew
what greatness was to be unleashed on them as the celestial bodies
of Coquihani and the sun collided.

After their time spent in the observatory, both men were covered in salty sweat. They guzzled water while seated on the steps of
the palace, watching the crowd grow in size and temperament. The
plaza was alive with humanity. The king and queen waved from the
palace to the inhabitants of their great kingdom. Dawn, and with
it Coquihani, would be coming for Beedxe'. Danaà and Beedxe'
ascended the steps to the palace for regal blessings.

As they reached the top of the steps, King Kasakir addressed
them. "Stand beside me Beedxe'," he motioned as if requesting; he
was not. "I would like to wish you well before your journey. Some
call it a transformation, the queen and I prefer journey." Apparently,
the king was cautiously beginning with small talk. Though the
residents of his great city didn't know what all the fuss was about,
they did know that Coquihani must be appeased.

"Can you feel the beast? Do you feel anger? Fear? Despair?
Please, speak freely." There was generosity in his eyes, something
Beedxe' thought forbidden to the great king. Kings must always
project strength as it helps garner fear. Fear is a very useful tool used
by leaders to command obedience.

"I feel anger. I feel hunger. I have never been angry by nature,
but I feel it swelling through my core." He had thrown caution to
the wind and decided not to hold back from the king. "I can only
hope to control the urge to hunt until after I have left the city."

"I am sure you will. In case you do not, there is no dishonor
in it. The beast will have its way. Between the two of us, I do not
think the jaguar prefers the flesh of men. You must merely embrace

the change; the spirit of the jaguar will take its course. Those who have wisdom will stay clear of the beast, if not …" A long stare and steady nod accompanied his advice.

Beedxe' returned the nod and showed the queen a submissive bow, which she gracefully returned. "Coquihani smile upon you Beedxe'. Here, this will help calm you." She handed him a piece of the sweet cactus treat they had gifted her mere hours before.

Maybe that childish smile wasn't gone just yet, he showed it along with a blush while thanking her for the gift. "Thank you, my queen. You are too kind."

With that, Beedxe' made his way back to Danaà who jokingly put a fist to the nagual's cheek as if punching. A strange, child-like smile had found its way to Danaà's face. "This is your moment Beedxe', not mine. Embrace that thought while you snack on your morsel. We now return to the altar and on to your acceptance from Coquihani." They shared a nod as Beedxe' slowly nibbled.

A hush moved over the crowd as the two descended down the stairs and to the altar. The moment was near, and something was sure to excite them. "Another sip of tonic for luck? Not that you need it." Danaà offered more of the moonflower drink. "Just a sip now, too much and the light will hurt your eyes."

Beedxe' took a sip from the flask and handed it back to Danaà. "I feel him Danaà, he is coming."

"I can feel him too, he reveals himself in your eyes. Dawn is breaking, it is time to release him. Look now, into the fire."

Beedxe' felt his bones bending. Crushing pain overwhelmed his jaws where he felt large canines forming in the front of his mouth, tormented in their need rip and tear flesh. His molars became enlarged, jagged and sharp. Eyes became fiercely dominant, while whiskers erupted through his cheeks.

Groaning in the pleasure of his pain he was on all fours now. A tail sprouted like a liana vine from his rear, and fur devoured his skin. Screaming now, as claws sharper than obsidian blades tore through the toes of what was now four feet. Hissing and roaring, the jaguar was revealed, and the bright light of Coquihani himself burst upon the beast and spread across the Oaxaca.

Roaring with intoxicating exhilaration, delightfully frightened city folk took a knee and braced themselves as the beast moved among them. They were electrified by the spectacle of transformation, yet hopeful the jaguar craved anything but their flesh. The great uija-tào moved forward, grabbed Beedxe's priestly robe and threw it into the fire of the altar. Dark grey smoke clouded the area and spread like a fog guiding the jaguar to the city's edge and to freedom.

With Cocijo's blessing by night, followed by Coquihani's blessing at dawn, the cloud people received a double invocation of benediction. The transcendence of Beedxe' was *not* myth, *not* legend, but ordained by the god of light himself.

• • •

BLACK JAGUARS WERE UNCOMMON IN THE OAXACA. THE ABSENCE of tree shade forced the adaptation of a predominantly yellow pigmentation of the fur, this yellow was accented with black to scatter the visions of unsuspecting prey. Beedxe', however, was no common jaguar.

Colored the deepest shade of black and masked by the will of the gods, Beedxe' was now free to roam the dry and rocky floor of the Oaxaca basin. While the beast within him hungered for violence, the newly minted nagual felt the urge to run. What good was agility and speed if one was unable to test it?

He ran and leapt and snarled. Hissing and roaring at the risen sun in recognition of the light god who provided him with transcendence. One more celebratory roar, loud and proud; now bring on the hunt!

Rows upon rows of organ pipe cacti sprouted from the ground in scattered lines. Twice as tall as a man, these cacti provided a false sense of protection for the creatures inhabiting their shadows. The sun tickled the tops of the cacti casting a cooling shade down one side of the plant and then the other. Prowling through this shade was the jaguar inhabited by the young Beedxe'.

Ears erect and listening for danger, the Tehuantepec jackrabbit is munching away on its breakfast. Feasting on sagebrush, this mammoth of a rabbit stands nearly two feet tall. He wears a fur jacket colored brown and accented by a white breast. He is decorated with stripes of black streaking down his backside and the black dot of a fuzzy tail; simply put-delicious!

Beedxe' embraces the beast's hunting instinct and allows the jaguar he inhabits to take control. Creeping to the right of the cacti, so as to remain camouflaged by the shade, he moves stealthily. Heart pounding and jaws drooling, the beast edges closer and closer still.

Pausing behind a large cactus directly behind his meal, the jaguar crouches and prepares the leaping assault to come. Then, as if catapulted by the rocks beneath his paws, the jaguar leaps into the air and pounces viciously upon the unsuspecting prey. Canines anchor into bone as muscle powered jaws crush the skull of the rabbit.

Blood flows as the jaguar licks at the salty plasma before devouring its flesh. Though not the tamandua Beedxe' was permitted to taste through his spiritual hunt, this kill is his and his alone.

• • •

THE FOLLOWING DAY, AFTER PRAISING AND PLEASING THEIR GODS, Danaà led Ayotli and a small caravan of pilgrims back to Lyobaa. These pilgrims were a mixed group of merchants, farmers and would be priests. They traveled back to the religious center of the cloud people looking for opportunity, blessings and a chance to see the return of the nagual.

Each passing patch of trees or shrubs now drew attention as they all craved a view of the jaguar containing the spirit of their beloved young priest. The journey home could be completed in a day with proper pace, having no need to stop for any religious purposes.

Beedxe' would return to Lyobaa in a few days, standing upright, eyes forever changed. In time, Beedxe's story of transformation would bring more and more people to Lyobaa. There has always been a need in men and women alike to search for signs of the gods, or at least to meet those who have been truly blessed by them.

PART TWO

CHAPTER 6

Summer 2003
Fort Sill, Oklahoma

Fort Sill, established in 1869, was once just a mere camp in the middle of what was then Native American Indian territory. Considered to be the last active frontier post, it now boasts itself as the home of the field artillery. The surroundings are still populated by many Native American peoples in the area; most commonly the Kiowa, Comanche, and Apache inhabit the immediate vicinity.

While today's Fort Sill does not command, imprison nor combat the indigenous people; it stands as a relic of the deeds, and often misdeeds, of imperfect men. History, and judgments of that history, remain harsh yet hushed. There are no apologies to be given or taken, as we are not our ancestors. We are, however, imperfect men and women just as they were.

A black sedan predominantly marked with a red flag bearing two stars marked the commander of the field artillery's vehicle. Inside that vehicle rode Major General Percival and Agent Hamilton. Agent Hamilton was on strict orders, orders that General Percival would provide him the means to execute. The vehicle, driven by a young commissioned officer, parked along the curb in front of what was referred to as the Gunnery Department. Artillery minds were shaped into fine instruments of warfare here, a treasure trove of knowledge.

"I still don't understand why an artillery sergeant in an instructor capacity would be needed for an international mission." General Percival was partly being intentionally imprudent, and partly wondering exactly why agent Hamilton really wanted an audience with one of his soldiers.

"Honestly sir, I would share more with you if I could. Orders. I'm sure you understand." Staying respectful while keeping much needed secrets was an art form in and of itself.

"OK, I get it. I'll make your introduction to the first sergeant; the commander is observing training out in the sticks today. After that, I'll return to my office, where I'll wait for your briefing. Keep in mind, this is still my installation. Orders or not, you're my guest and you will give me an out brief." Bravado shot from the general's mouth as if a projectile from a howitzer.

"I wouldn't dream of leaving without saying goodbye, sir." A wink and a smile and they exited the sedan. Walking down the sidewalk from the car to the building, soldiers were already standing at the position of attention and rendering salutes. General Percival was a well built, fifty-something man. He stood fairly tall with perfect posture. His hair was a peppered grey and his faced was shaved as slick as a whistle. Hamilton, on the other hand was short and stout; resembling an upright bulldog with human ears, though clean shaven. His skin was a natural tan color.

The soldiers held their salutes until returned by their commander. Salutes remain an intricate part of military discipline as well as being a vehicle for demonstrating respect. As his soldiers delivered salutes with respect, they were returned with an equal amount of enthusiasm and respect. Hamilton smiled and nodded as the commanding officer returned salutes and greeted his men and women.

"In the door and to the left!" The commander said. It was always good as a leader to ensure your comrades knew where they were headed.

"BATTERY, ATTEN-TION." The building was quickly called to attention when its commanding general entered, also a long-standing tradition.

"Carry on!" General Percival announced, "carry on!" He stopped to have a few brief words with his soldiers; a leader always has to have a feel for the pulse of his or her fighting force. Direct communication from commander to soldier effectively accomplished this. "Now, stay with me Agent Hamilton."

They took another left into the door of what was referred to as the orderly room. Before the first sergeant could call the room to attention, General Percival waved the group of soldiers off. "As you were," The general commanded. "I'm afraid I only have a use for you Top." Hint taken, the first sergeant immediately dispensed of everyone else in the room. Agent Hamilton took the liberty of closing the door.

"This is Agent Hamilton." Hamilton and the top shook hands. "He needs to have a word with Staff Sergeant Patee. I'm afraid that's all the information we can give you right now. Good enough?"

"Yes sir! You're the boss!" The first sergeant knew it wasn't really a question or option. Thirty-five and going on fifty, the first sergeant appeared to have a lot of "extra mileage". Greyed hair and wrinkles should not decorate a man of his age. A razor-sharp glance and a permanently mounted scowl demanded respect from his subordinates.

"Actually, the agent man here's the boss for now. Make sure Patee knows this is no request." General Percival said looking back to Agent Hamilton. "I'll speak to you soon." The two nodded and the general motioned again for them to relax. As he exited the building, the command of attention was again given. "Carry on" he announced, as he was on his way.

"I really must apologize, I know this is awkward. I wouldn't be here if it weren't absolutely necessary." The agent looked to calm the tension which was obviously present between them.

"I suppose it won't do me any good to ask what this is about? I'm sure you can understand, my joes are my responsibility," the first sergeant said.

Noticing a puzzled look on the agent's face, the first sergeant went on to explain that artillery leaders often referred to their soldiers as joes; no doubt a play on words. The general gist behind it? The large bullets fired by the howitzers, called projectiles, were commonly referred to as projos; a simple derivative of this term, joes, was a fitting moniker for the soldiers firing them.

"Sorry, orders." Agent Hamilton liked to keep things as short as possible with those uninvolved, it tended to be the most effective way to guard classified information without being disrespectful.

"Follow me then. He's just down the hall, rehearsing." The first sergeant slapped him on the back of the shoulder briskly, and off they went. They followed a bricked wall corridor decorated with unit awards and plaques commemorating the deeds of the unit's soldiers, past and present. "If you have time, take a look around the installation while you're here. Good or bad, there's a lot of history

here; Geronimo, Satanta, Quanah Parker, you name it!" Pointing
to the door they were about to enter, "I guess it's time to make
sergeant Patee's day."

Looking in through the window of the door, they could see
the young staff sergeant writing on a dry erase board and speaking
to an invisible audience. "Rehearsal sucks," top said as they peered
through the small window, "but it's necessary."

Top quietly opened the door to a crack, allowing them to hear
the rehearsal before interrupting. He heard Patee pitching straight
from the lesson plan. "Vertical angle is nothing more than difference
in altitude between two points ..." The first sergeant flung the door
open quickly, breaking the instructor's concentration.

"Perfect! I almost had that part down top." Standing there all of
about a hundred and fifty pounds, obviously of Hispanic descent;
Patee was of an average size and build, but his smile could break
the ice of a glacier. Agent Hamilton was almost sure he was joking.

"Top?! Do I look like I stand on my head and spin, staff sergeant?" The first sergeant smirked, holding back a smile that soon
burst on his face like a splat of mud.

"Hahaha, do you really want me to answer that?" He chuckled,
half searching for amusement on the salty face of the first shirt.

"Never mind all that." Shaking his hand and lowering his laughter back to a growl. "This is Agent Hamilton. You've been directed
to speak with Agent Hamilton, and to be accommodating to whatever he is here for. Understand, General Percival gave me the orders
I give you." Looking around the room, and back at the drawing on
the board, he said, "It does look like you're making progress. Let
me know if you two need anything and, uh, don't worry, I'll get the

door." The sarcastic smile thrown at Sergeant Patee was meant to show his lack of approval concerning the current situation.

Once he was past the door and down the hall Agent Hamilton began. "Let's have a seat, huh? We have a lot to talk about, and I'm afraid our conversation stays between us, understood?"

"Yes sir." The sergeant took a seat, leaned forward and leered at Hamilton as if compelling him to get on with it.

Agent Hamilton took a plain folder out of his briefcase and a pen from his suit's jetted pocket. "OK, let's get the obvious out of the way. You are Staff Sergeant Citalli Patee, correct?"

"Yes."

"You are from Beyulu, Florida. Did I say that right?"

"Yes, I am," smiling, "and yes, you did."

Agent Hamilton set the pen and folder down. "Citalli, that's an interesting name. It must have some origin ... some meaning?"

"My mother and father immigrated from Mexico before I was born. It's a traditional name, she always maintained that it meant star. I would joke 'hey, I'm going to be a star'. She was always so serious, so naturally, she got upset." He said a bit uncomfortably, remembering his mother's ire.

Hamilton, now catching on to the sergeant's quirky sense of humor tilted his head and smiled. "She didn't want you to be a star?"

"The name refers to a star, you know, in the sky. It's a name that has been given exclusively to daughters, not sons. My mother was so adamant about the fact that I was her little star that she threw out the notion of gender specific names. I guess even the most ancient of cultures can evolve. Our people, well, you wouldn't understand." Why should he be giving information before he gets a little, he thought. "What about you, agent man? It might help break the ice a little if I had a first name to go by. Or is that too bold?"

"Gustavo, well … Gus. Call me Gus. Believe it or not, we'll be working closely together; so Citalli, my name is Gus. That better?"

"A little I suppose. Do you intend on getting to the point, Gus?"

To the point! Conversations just seemed more productive when direct communication was applied. Gus, also, just sounded so much better than Agent Hamilton.

"To the point then." Picking the pen back up and twirling it between his fingers while searching for the most direct way to move forward. "We know your parents immigrated from Mexico, but you've probably figured that out."

"I have. But a little honesty always helps break the ice." Citalli was moving his hand in a circular motion in front of his chest, egging Gus on to keep going.

"Your parents are from Oaxaca, Mexico. Your father came to help during rebuilding efforts caused by Hurricane Agnes in 1972. After repairs were completed the following year he requested, and received, a work visa. 1974 your mother moved to the city of Beyulu, Florida; and that's where you and your brother were born. Your brother, Cayo, still resides there to this day. Correct?"

"Seems like you know me about as well as I know myself." Citalli laughed, wondering where in the world this was going.

"You're married now, spouse is of Native American ethnicity, and is nine months pregnant."

"OK, OK. Where are we going with this?" Citalli was beginning to think time was up on the formalities. No need to answer endless questions on yourself.

"To the point then, sorry," Agent Hamilton said, feeling his welcome dissipating. "We have reason to believe that the ancient peoples of the Oaxaca, specifically the Zapotec, developed a very powerful weapon. We have reason to believe that one or more of the cartels south of our border will attempt to extract this weapon from its current location."

"And that has what to do with me? I am an artilleryman, not exactly trained for guerilla warfare. Well, I have some training, but nothing that couldn't be trumped by special forces, or even delta force. Why me? Heck, I don't even know that area outside of what my mother told me about it, and the only language I speak is English. So ..." Understandably, Citalli was confused when it came to the intent here.

"The CIA, Department of the Interior and Department of State are all in agreement that this must be stopped. Right or wrong, good or bad, your name has been submitted to be part of this mission. You are a soldier, aren't you?"

Gus was starting to come off a little coy here, and Citalli would have none of it. Just because there were orders involved, did not mean you followed them blindly.

"An effective soldier is an informed soldier. I mean, listen, my wife is due any day. You want me to charge off to the Oaxaca region with that train wreck of a story? Is that where we are? Get a grip!" Humor was sucked out of the room like air through jet engine.

Agent Hamilton paused, looked down and right, searching for a solid response. He looked back up at the sergeant, "do you know what a clairvoyant is, Citalli?"

Obviously, this conversation was going sideways. "Of course, I know what a clairvoyant is. Are you telling me a fortune teller dictated my presence? I mean, I heard the CIA was a dream job; but I never thought you actually dreamed ON the job."

"I'm not talking about fortune telling sergeant, and the United States government does not pay me to sleep on the job. Listen," Gus leaned back in his chair, "it's me, ok, I'm the clairvoyant. And I'm here speaking with you because this was my vision, and because you were in it."

"How does that work exactly? You 'dream a little dream'," Citalli said using his fingers to mark the quotations, "and suddenly we have an international incident? OK, fine, what number am I thinking about?"

"You're obviously being more than a little cynical, but I'm not pulling your leg here. Your own people had this gift, why would it be so impossible for me to have it? You cannot tell me you doubt the legends of your own people." Gus seemed genuinely upset at Citalli's skepticism.

Citalli saw what he believed to be genuine anger in Gus's facial expressions. Maybe he was being serious. Those feelings aside, Citalli actually did believe. Not because some federal agent's ramblings, but because his mother convinced him it was true. Citalli believed in the old ways because of her teachings, and because he still conversed with her in his prayers. Those prayers to his mother, now deceased, were real. There was a mystical realm, there was no denying that.

"I do believe in mysticism but abhor when people refer to it as the occult. We're not talking cults here, are we?"

"No, Citalli. No cults, and certainly no crystal balls." He paused for a moment, trying to transition into the mission. All things considered, the conversation had actually gone very well. "Look, I know this seems like an impossibly crazy idea. Powerful weaponry of this nature being made some two thousand years ago. To be quite honest with you, we're not exactly sure what we're dealing with here."

Now Citalli was confused again. "I thought you had visions? I was under the impression you were the real deal. How about you tell me about the *whole* vision."

"What I was hoping, if we're trying to be honest here, was an invite to your home. Now, before you say anything; I just think we should discuss this way out in the sticks. There would be far fewer distraction, and no need to worry about eavesdropping. What say we discuss this over a beer?" Gus hoped he wasn't being too bold too soon.

"That's the smartest thing you've said all day," Citalli said. "We just need to stop by the orderly room so I can let top know we're out for the day."

Checking out was quick and easy. After all, top was under orders to comply with all of the agent's needs. As for Citalli, he needed a break from talking to four walls and empty chairs. While rehearsal was akin to self-administered punishment, it was completely necessary.

Driving with the windows down about 30 miles north of Fort Sill, Gus and Citalli were tasting that first ice cold beer already. Funny how it tickled the taste buds without even being opened.

"This is a really nice roadrunner, Citalli. Is she a seventy-two?" Gus asked, referring to Citalli's beautiful car.

"Nineteen and seventy-one, she belonged to my dad. He wanted the seventy-two until they sprung the news on him: no Hemi. Anyway, she's something else, huh?" Citalli loved to brag on his ride.

"So, it's all original? Even this beautiful blue color?"

"Yup! Sure is, especially the paint. It's called moon indigo, dad loved the color. I call it 'blue'." With most of the unpleasantness out of the way, Citalli's quirky sense of humor was coming back.

"There certainly aren't many trees out this way are there?" Gus seemed disappointed. "I mean, I've got it, this was the prairie, the last frontier. Still though, come on, it needs trees!"

"Now, there's something we can agree on. Florida had so many trees. I still miss home, but hey, Army life, you know. Anyway, we're here."

"So, besides home, what do you call this place? We're not exactly in town," Gus said, overstating the obvious.

"Taugui, and no, you're not going to find the name on a map, but we call it Taugui. Really only the locals would know what you're talking about if you say Taugui," Citalli said.

"Interesting name, any origin?" Indigenous studies were Gus's forte, especially when those studies were Mesoamerican.

"Something about when the Apache and Kiowa originally co-inhabited the area. Loosely translated it means sitting outside," Citalli was reciting truths as he understood them at the time.

Entering the driveway, Gus observed what was a dry, grassy plot just off the beaten path. They drove down a gravel driveway to a small white wooden house. It wasn't much to look at, but home was home.

"So, you did call your wife and tell her company was coming, didn't you?" Gus had his polite guest face on.

"I did, but she's at her mom's. The closer we get to being parents, the more she needs a mother," Citalli said, laughing sheepishly. "Anyway, she'll be pretty upset that I have to leave. Speaking of which, how long are we planning to be gone?"

"If all goes as expected, two or three days. We'll get to that, but yeah, shouldn't be long at all."

"Let's grab a couple of cold ones from the cooler and take a walk, I'll give you the grand tour." Citalli grabbed two plastic grocery bags from the car (one for full cans, and one for empties), tossed a few beers in one of them, and handed a cold one to Gus. A smile and a nod followed by a metallic snap and the hissing of the cans opening, now they were getting somewhere!

Citalli pointed his right hand upwards toward the sky, made a circular motion, "Let's move out. Besides, I can't believe we only got a twelve pack; that's not enough to get me started on a bad day!"

Patee was smiling more now and laughing, maybe there was a bond growing between the two, or maybe, he just wanted to get hammered, thought Gus.

CHAPTER 7

"CHEERS, GUSTAVO, SECRET AGENT MAN!" THERE WAS THAT GOOFY smile on Citalli's face again.

"Cheers."

The two of them quietly walked down an easterly path, to a poor little excuse for a pond.

"What, are you nursing that one?" Citalli teased, washing down the reminder of his beer. He crushed the can and placed it in the spare bag, grabbing two more and gesturing. "While they're cold, huh?"

Gus knocked back the rest of his beer then, crushing the can, traded the old for a new. "Thanks. Take it kind of easy, tomorrow's going to be a long day."

"Whoa! Tomorrow? Already? Nothing like waiting until the last minute to get started." Citalli seemed more amused than upset, chalk it up to military humor. "Here's the deal: if we're going to be marauding off into the great unknown together, you need to relax a little. I mean, come on, we're in the boondocks now. Put that tie in your pocket, maybe unbutton that suffocating top button. Even if it doesn't help you, it'll help me feel so much better."

"I guess you've got a point. After all, it's hot out here in the direct sunlight." Tie off and in his jacket pocket, Gus unbuttoned the top two buttons of his shirt. He then continued to take off his jacket and flop it over his shoulder. "Better?"

"Much," joked Citalli downing another beer "there's two more, get with it!"

Hoping this wasn't a sign of things to come, Gus made quick work of his beer, then accepted another.

"That's my corn growing over there on the other side of the pond. I plant and harvest my own corn. It's going to be some fall harvest this year!" Citalli spoke matter-of-factly now. "I know it seems kind of goofy, but my mother insisted on having a small garden and corn was a must; maize was, and still is, essential to our people. I do it in remembrance of her. Of course, it doesn't hurt that I really like fresh corn, too," Citalli said.

"I think that's great, really I do. By the way ... forty-seven."

"Huh?" Citalli seemed stunned by the random number.

"Forty-seven, that's the number you were thinking, wasn't it?"

"Hah! Yes! I thought you said, 'it doesn't work like that'," Citalli said imitating Gus's demure nature.

"Well, you can't expect a whole lot when you're being so apprehensive, can you?" Smiling now, Gus was teasing and opening up some.

"Yeah, I shouldn't be like that, but you were spewing all kinds of crap. You're hard to get a read on."

"I needed to establish a little rapport with you before going into specifics. You understand?" The two shared a nod. "You might need to drink one or two more before the rest of the story."

"Fair enough," Citalli gestured his best *follow me* motion. "Let's do that on the back porch."

As the two men headed back to the house, Citalli motioned Gus to have a seat on the porch while he retrieved the rest of the beer from the car. When he made it back to the porch, he noticed Gus had already crushed his can in preparation for another.

"Now you're catching on! Don't worry, you can crash in the spare room. That way you can just ride with me back to work in the morning; cool?" Citalli raised a single eyebrow as if questioning Gus.

"Yeah, I guess that works. I can already feel a buzz coming on, so I don't think either of us should drive. Obviously, I'm not the professional you are," Gus ribbed.

"It takes practice," laughing with approval, "but I really don't drink much anymore. Getting married, then prepping for father-hood, I guess it kinda took the wild side out of me. I feel I might need a little of that wild side where we're going."

"Well, it should comfort you to know that I'm not much of a field agent, then. Like I said, I'm a clairvoyant. We'll be taking two field agents with us tomorrow. I'll make the introductions when you meet them; make sense?"

"None of this makes sense. The ancestors were simple people with powerful ways. They drew their powers from the gods, not from some ancient weapon of mass destruction," Citalli quipped.

"There it is! I was wondering when you might open up. You're familiar with the old ways, aren't you? I guess the real question might be: are you simply aware of the old ways, or do you practice them? I mean, I just have this feeling that you're a lot more into your ancestral ways than you let on."

Citalli smiled in acknowledgement, "Some, but with your gifts, you should understand. Look, when people see things as being different, they get, I don't know, unpredictable. I don't exactly practice sacrifice and blood-letting, you know."

"Good to know!" The two of them shared an honest laugh together. "I guess I should stop messing around and tell you about the vision," he cleared his throat, "my vision."

"I'm all ears," Citalli joked nervously, pushing his earlobes forward jokingly and thinking it was about time.

"The original vision I had was when I was visiting the ruins at Monte Albàn a few weeks ago. I was there on a vacation, I love Mesoamerican history. I placed my hand on what they refer to now as mound J, or building J. It's believed to be an old observatory."

"My mother used to talk about it," Citalli offered, "and yes, it's an observatory."

"Good to know, from someone with actual knowledge," Gus replied. "Anyway, when I touched the stone surface of the building, I saw the attack. Well, maybe not an attack. More like an attempted theft. Do you know what a conquest slab is?"

"Yes," Citalli answered, "the observatory is decorated with them. Basically, they represent fallen or conquered enemies. All in the name I guess."

"Again, correct," Gus concentrated and looked as if he was seeing the events again in his mind. "Whatever they were trying to take was concealed behind one of those slabs, on the south side. That's when I clearly saw your face. You were in uniform, and I clearly saw the patch on your shoulder and of course, I saw your name tape. How many Patee's are in the army with that patch, huh?"

"OK. Well that explains why me. But that doesn't explain a powerful weapon." Citalli was trying to digest as much as he could.

"That's when I saw it. The brightest light I have ever seen. Blinding, like sunlight, or a nuke, maybe. The point is, we have to be sure. I've honestly never seen anything like it." Gus paused and regathered himself. "After a couple of weeks of this dominating my dreams I was able make out an approximate date, within a day. Sorry, best I could do."

"Is this standard data for you guys? I mean, I understand you have a gift, but the government is going to fund this? No disrespect."

"It's a small, short operation. We think we can handle it with little to no casualties, not to mention minimal staffing. We're going to attempt to capture the thieves, you know, catch them in the act. We'd like to know exactly what's in there before choosing any course of action. We don't want to cause any undue damage to historical sites. So, that's what I've got; that's the mission. I'll hold a more in-depth briefing with the whole team covering all the particulars during the flight down. I'll tell your commander, General Percival, everything he needs to know in the morning."

"I'll be the one to tell Kara, my wife, later this evening; after dinner," Citalli said as if now in agreement with the mission.

"I was hoping dinner was in the plans."

"Well, she's supposed to be home at six," Glancing at his watch, "and she's late again. I guess I would be surprised if she was ever early," Citalli said with husband-like affection.

As they walked through the house to the front door, a small white car pulled in the driveway. "Must have known we were talking about her," Citalli said smiling. He flung the door open with a loving smile on his face, "Late again!"

"Hey," she returned the smile, "Mom and I were cooking your dinner, goofball!"

She stood all but about five foot three, skin and bones, but with a big belly. Obviously, she was slightly more than just a little pregnant.

Citalli jotted out to carry dinner in for Kara. Placing his arm around her, "Kara, I would like you to meet Gus Hamilton. Gus, this is Kara." He waved his hand back and forth to accentuate mutual greetings and hellos were exchanged between the two.

"I smell beer! Is this some kind of party or something?" She said jokingly, but half perturbed.

"I'm afraid we're not celebrating a damn thing. I mean, darn thing." He said, making amends for his use of profanity. "Let's just get to grubbing, I'll tell you about it after dinner."

"OK," she said, "but this doesn't sound good!"

"C'mon, Let's just chill out and eat. You're in no condition to be upset." Citalli was poking at her protruding belly. "Happy thoughts for our little bundle of joy."

The three of them proceeded into the house, where Mom's home cooking had finally made it to the table. "How about a bottle of water to wash that down?" Citalli said, making a suggestion. "It's hot outside and we could all use a little hydration."

"Sounds perfect to me," Gus announced, "besides, we're out of beer."

"So, you have a suit and not a uniform, Gus. What is it you do for a living?" Kara sensed something different … call it military spouse intuition.

"Well, not to get you too alarmed, but I'm a federal agent. Your husband and I will be working together for a few days." Gus wanted to be polite to Citalli, who insisted on telling his wife in his own time. His own time being only a few more short hours.

"Gustavo, well, Gus, is here on official business. Because of the nature of his business, I thought it would be best if he stayed with us tonight. It's giving us the opportunity to get comfortable around each other, plus I needed that beer like you could not believe!" He said, laughing, knowing Kara was not amused in the slightest.

Dinner wrapped up and Citalli took Kara for a walk. It was cooler now, and they could use the privacy. Cicadas, frogs, and crickets sent music adrift upon the winds. The soothing stir of near silence accented by nature was enough to calm just about anyone. Kara, Citalli thought, may need a little more than the soothing sounds of creation to keep her cool. A military wife, Kara was used to an occasional deployment or training exercise, but with the baby on the way, it would be ideal to have her husband home with her.

His plan seemingly had worked to perfection as the two returned from their walk. Looking as though he'd accomplished the impossible, Citalli smiled widely and announced, "It's official, you're in trouble, Gus!" Smiling and trying to break the obvious tension.

"No," Kara said, "you're not in trouble, but you better take care of him. He's going to be a father any time now, and it's your responsibility to bring him home. Got it?"

"Yes Ma'am!" Gus was quick to announce. That was much quicker and easier than he would have thought. Even in the military community, planning was preferred. "This should be a relatively short operation. Truly though, I feel like I owe you an apology for the terrible timing. I know we're asking a lot."

CHAPTER 8

UP AND AT 'EM AT FIVE IN THE MORNING, CITALLI AND GUS HEADED back to Fort Sill. "I called your CG, General Percival, last night; just go straight to headquarters." Gus informed Citalli as they entered the installation.

"Okie dokie, you're the boss! Was he upset you didn't stop by yesterday?"

"A little, I suppose. He'll get over it, just like I'll get over this hangover. We all take orders, staff sergeant." Gus replied as if Citalli needed a reminder.

Pulling the car up to headquarters, Citalli noticed a couple of serious looking gents that appeared to be waiting in front of the building. "Is that your crew there?"

"That would be them alright. I think you'll like them, they're both prior enlisted, though neither was artillery." Gus figured army was army, but each branch kind of has their own way about them, not to mention their own jargon. In any case, the three of them would all have enlisted army service in common. They all seemed to have an atypical sense of humor about them too. Gus couldn't help but to wonder whether or not that was issued with their uniforms. "Just stop right here in front and jump out. I'll introduce you."

"Yup-yup," Citalli confirmed.

Citalli parked the car and the two of them jumped out of the vehicle and approached the two men. Introductions were made, and bravado filled handshakes were exchanged. The first of the two, Garcia, was a tall, lanky bearded man. He appeared all of twenty-five years old but looked as if he could snatch a man's heart out with little effort. Ramirez, the second of the two, was a little older looking, maybe mid-thirties. His face was pitted and decorated with a slender, well-groomed moustache. He had a lean, muscular build and was just a tad shorter than his battle buddy.

"As you can tell," Gus began to explain, "We like to blend into our environment. We're going to Mexico, so it helps to have people of Hispanic ethnicity. No room for affirmative action in foreign countries, you either blend in, or you don't."

"Makes sense," Citalli agreed, "Let's get this show on the road, then."

"Tell you what," Gus said, "give these two a ride over to the airstrip, and I'll meet you there when I'm done briefing the CG." Looking now at Garcia and Ramirez, "You two got everything ready to roll?"

"Please," Ramirez quipped, "we stay ready!"

"Yeah, yeah, yeah … I got it. See you in a few." Gus pretended to tip a hat that wasn't there.

"Nice car," Garcia stated ogling at the set of wheels in front of them. "Am I driving?"

"Oh, you have jokes?" Citalli could tell right away they would get along. "You a car junky?"

"Nah, I just like to drive fast. Admiring cars, that's more Ramirez's style."

"You got that right!" Ramirez said in admiration of the car. "Somebody put some love into this one. I don't suppose you'd want to sell it, would you? I'll make you a good offer; always loved these cars."

"Sorry, no. It was my father's pride and joy, he willed it to me when he passed, and …"

"Say no more," Ramirez stopped him right there. "Car's speak to people, speak about people. This car, it means more than metal, plastic and rubber to you. She's a beaut!"

In the car and down the road they went. Parking on the north side of the airstrip where the vehicle could sit unbothered for a few days. They boarded a sleek Dassault Falcon Fifty aircraft, strikingly fancy for a government jet. They had been shooting the breeze a mere five or ten minutes when Gus came on board.

"Well, that was fast!" Ramirez started. "Did you kiss him goodbye?"

"Hardy har har, thousands of comedians out of work and I get this guy! CG just wanted the common courtesy and respect of knowing what was going on. So naturally, I told him what he needed to know," he shot a sarcastic looking grin Citalli's way. "Let's get this thing in the air, huh?" Gus was ready get this little mission started and ended as soon as he could. He was never one to cut corners, but he didn't like wasting precious time either.

Once they reached a nice cruising altitude of about forty-thousand feet, Gus unbuckled his seatbelt, "Let's go over a short briefing while we're in the air, huh? Here, just a few photos of our area of operations. Try to commit them to memory as best you can. Our area of operations will be relatively small. Still, best to know your surroundings."

He passed a folder containing a set of numbered photos to each of them. They were seated in a set of four wide, beige-leather seats. There was one seat on either side of the narrow aisle with each one facing the another, such a convenience for small briefings.

"As you all know by now, these pictures are of the ruins at the historical site at Monte Albàn in Oaxaca, Mexico. Beginning with the first photo, which is the one on top, Garcia." A little chuckle amongst the group helped break the ice. "You'll notice all of the ancient structures are pretty much running in straight lines, except one; it kinda looks like it doesn't belong. This is what's referred to as 'Building J' or 'The Observatory'." He looked around and made sure all the men identified the correct structure.

"You'll also notice stairs going up the north-east side of the building, and these doorways along the south side. The large set of stairs directly to the south of the observatory go up what we refer to as the south platform. Contact is expected to be made in this plaza area between the south platform and the observatory. More specifically, we expect the perps to target the area behind one of these carvings. The carvings are what are referred to as conquest slabs, got it?"

"So, we still plan to let the thieves attempt to take what they came for, boss?" Ramirez confirmed.

"Yes, there's been a lot of apprehension surrounding that, but yeah. What we want to do is to let them identify which slab the weapon is concealed behind, then intercept them before any damage is done to the structure. You'll notice two doors along this side of the structure; well, one on either side of this angled corner. Garcia and Ramirez, you're going to be located at the southernmost door, here." Gus instructed pointing at the doorway. "Citalli, you and I will be inside this other doorway."

"So, do we think we at least know what time of night these knuckleheads will be trying to pull this off?" Garcia asked.

"My best guess, and I'm usually really close, is right about dawn. But if we're going to have the element of surprise, well, it looks as if we'll be spending the night."

"Ooh, maybe we'll get lucky and see some ghosts!" Ramirez joked.

"Any ghosts and I'm out," said Citalli, "you guys will be on your own! Nobody said a thing about ghosts!"

The group shared a good long laugh at Citalli's expense. He smiled and giggled along, not quite sure himself if he was joking or not.

"Agent Hamilton," said Ramirez, rejecting any form of first name informalities. "You're quite sure this is the man you saw in your vision?" Motioning now to Citalli, "Sergeant Patee, you sure you're up to this?" It was meant as a joke, but one that required an answer, not from Citalli, but from the boss man.

"Positive, Ramirez. It may also calm your nerves to know that his ancestors are descended from this area. His parents moved to the United States in 1972 from here. These are his people." Gus was trying his best to justify Citalli's involvement, though he knew there was no need.

"Alright, as long as you're sure. Please don't take this personally, Sergeant, but I don't think this type of mission is suited to your training is it?"

"Probably not," Citalli replied, "but I can hold my own. You don't have to worry about that."

"Good!" Said Gus. "We'll talk more when we get on the ground. We still have a relatively short opportunity to catch a few winks. Nap time!"

The other three picked up on the opportunity for a quick nod and smartly got to it. It's amazing how soundly one sleeps on an airplane, as if floating amongst the clouds. Mission looming or not, a soldier can sleep just about anywhere.

After what seemed like a few minutes later to the sleeping task force, the plane landed at Xoxocotlán International Airport in Oaxaca, Mexico.

"Dude, it feels like I just fell asleep!" Garcia said, overstating the obvious. "Maybe I should've just stayed awake."

"Hopefully we'll have time for another wink or two before game time." Ramirez added, treating the whole scenario as if it were some form of trivial training exercise.

"We'll see, first we need to establish communications with our liaison, hopefully that liaison is here. Have the crew remove our coolers from the aircraft and have them ready for any inspections. Remember, transparency is a must!" Clearly, Gus was up to the challenge of taking charge. Their gear and weaponry were tucked into wheeled coolers so that they appeared as tourists.

The aircraft's stairs were lowered allowing its four occupants to exit. A short, unimposing man awaited them on the tarmac. Clearly an older man, he was wrinkled and accented by grey hair. He gave a brief wave, then ceremoniously motioned the group over.

"Do you speak English?" Gus asked up front.

"Yes. You must be Agent Hamilton." The man said in a thick Spanish accent.

"Yes sir! This is Ramirez, Garcia and Patee." Gus gestured at each of them and allowed for a brief hand shake.

"My name is Eduardo Nieto, I will escort you to Monte Albàn. Please, grab your gear and follow me."

Eduardo led them to a well-worn, green, unmarked minivan. "Best not to draw any attention, no?" He said in what was more of a cackle than a laugh. "Please, get in. From here it is about a thirty-minute drive to Monte Albàn. Will there be any need to stop on our way? Water? Dinner? Anything?"

"No, thank you. We just need to get on the ground and get a feel for everything before dark. We've brought ample food and water." Gus answered for the group.

They drove through a modest, but colorful city; admiring its simple beauty while remaining aware of its dangers. Deep in the heart of Sinaloa Cartel turf, this once peaceful city had become gripped with fear over its never-ending drug war. Simple people who wanted nothing more than to live in peace while raising their families, were forced to remain vigilant and submissive in order to survive. A modern reality that was a crime in and of itself.

After passing through the city they reached a long, mostly straight but uphill road leading them to the north side of the archeological complex. "Welcome to Monte Albàn, gentlemen. Tourist hours are not over yet, I could arrange a tour guide if you like, it would not be a problem." Eduardo offered up, though expecting to hear a quick 'no' from the group.

"Nah, I think we're good. I was just here not that long ago. Just to make sure we're all on the same sheet of music, there are no roving or walking guards tonight. Is that correct?" Gus was ready to get started.

"They usually make occasional roves, but those have been canceled tonight as you have requested. We have made every effort to ensure that no one is harmed."

"Great!" Gus said, "If you'd like, you can just drop us off at the visitor's center. We'll take it from there. Will you be remaining at the site all night?"

"Yes-yes, I will stay with the guard. Communicate to us whatever you see, or should you need anything, huh?"

"Absolutely, 'til then." The group exited the van, gathered their gear and made their way into the park. Eduardo motioned to the staff to let the group in. Entering the park, they made their way to the southern platform. Here they would have a great view of their area of operations, and an even better view of the coming sunset.

They made their way to the top of the steps leading up the platform, swung an immediate left and planted themselves promptly atop the grassy mound. One could see the whole valley from here. The men couldn't help but to think about how easy this must have been to defend. At the same time, this would have been a harsh environment to live in for the price of protection.

"Let's just cool out for a while and soak it all in. No shop talk until the tourists leave," said Gus.

"I've waited my whole life to see this," started Citalli. "To think men could level the top of a mountain, then create an architectural masterpiece like this! Of course, you guys are aware, many of the peoples in Mesoamerica enslaved their conquered captives. Ironic that the Spaniards would end up enslaving them in the same manner. Basically, the Spanish took the liberty of pulling off a massive snatch and grab with every precious resource they could find. Spoils of war I suppose. If not for those European diseases, heck, we might have had a chance."

"Easy with the preaching, my man. Everything happens for a reason. Progress is made whether we like it or not. These people were warriors, I'm not sure they would appreciate any excuses." Ramirez respected the aspects of war and conquest. More than that, he just kind of liked to have life wrapped up in a nice little package, bow on top and all.

"My father never really spoke of it. His views were similar to yours, just let sleeping dogs lie. My mother, on the other hand, was more of a tradionalist. She practiced the old ways." Citalli gave a hard and patriotic look to his comrades. "My people built this. These are our lands. My mother, like many of the Zapotec elders, believed the gods chose not to intervene. Maybe, and I know this sounds absurd, the gods were lulled to sleep. Unhappy with the people or something. Who knows?"

"You can't tell me you actually believe that, can you?" Garcia said skeptically. "You believe some pagan gods really ruled these lands? These gods that required bloodletting and human sacrifice? Come on guy, you don't believe that!"

"Garcia, I don't try to poke holes in Christianity. Why would you be so disrespectful to my ways? To answer your question, yes, I believe. I say my prayers to my ancestors and they answer. Are your prayers answered?"

Garcia took a deep breath, knowing he upset Citalli. "I don't mean to be insensitive, really I don't. I'm just completely blown away. I didn't know anyone still practiced those ways. I'm sorry buddy. Honestly, I apologize."

"It's ok," Citalli said lowering his tone. "I really don't talk about it, now you know why. I try to carry on my people's way and this site just talks to me. It says something about faith. People say faith can move mountains and here, right here, it did. Anyway, change of subject, please tell me we brought decent grub."

"Now you're talking," Gus let in. "We brought some sacked lunches and water, everything your little hearts desire! Not to mention a nine-millimeter sidearm with hip holster for dessert. The preferred method of engagement will be these tasers, though; remember, we need intel, and carcasses cannot provide a whole lot of that."

CHAPTER 9

NIGHT HAD FALLEN ON THE OAXACA, AND THE FOUR MEN SPLIT into their two designated pairs, one pair in each doorway. They spoke only in hushed tones and through in-ear tactical communication devices.

"OK guys, listen. One up and one down for the next couple of hours, then we're all up for the home stretch. Got it?" Gus waited for each of them to reply, then ordered radio silence. Turning his attention now to Citalli, "Before you sleep Citalli, I'm curious about something."

"Shoot! No, wait, don't shoot," he said laughingly. "I mean, ask your question."

"You don't like to use foul language. When you used some around your wife, you quickly recanted. Not to mention, after a look, she let you off the hook. What's up with that?"

"Oh, aren't we observant?" Laughing and making his eyes look big so as to mock Gus's attentiveness. "Kara and I decided that there would be no more foul language. We want to set a good example for the child. Funny, we won't even let them tell us the gender because, to us, it doesn't truly matter. What matters is that there is love, always love. Heck, she even told me I had to crack fewer jokes, but we settled on me telling cleaner jokes, educational jokes."

"Tell me one of those educational jokes, then."

"Haven't got any ready yet," Citalli said with a nervous grin. "I've still got a while after the baby's born until it can speak. That should give me some time to hone my skills."

"Ha, sometimes you're too much Citalli. Now, you nap first. Sleep."

Citalli smiled, pointed two fingers at his eyes then to Gus's. "Don't doze off, I may be watching."

After just a few seconds, Citalli looked up at Gus, "It's way too hot! Too hot to be thinking about sleep. I mean, the heat's one thing, but there's no wind getting into this cramped little room. Besides, while we're here, I have a few questions of my own, unless of course, you would rather take a quick nap."

Gus gave a chuckle, "I can never quite manage to sleep in this kind of heat either. Just drink some water and stay hydrated."

"Great! Fair's fair, you know," Citalli gave a smirk, "It's been all about me since we met. My turn to grill you for a while."

"Well, I guess when you're right, you're right. I really don't have much of a personal life, so don't worry about getting too personal."

"You're first name is Gustavo, last name Hamilton. You have a similar complexion to mine. What's your ethnicity?"

"Somehow, that always comes up. Everybody wants to know, or usually they just assume I can speak Spanish. Like you, I'm of Mexican descent. I have no idea what happened to my parents. I was adopted by an elderly Caucasian couple who wanted a child to love. I've often wondered about what my biological parents were like, or maybe what they did, or what happened. But when push comes to shove, I had love. I had a roof over my head, clothes on my back, and a sense of family."

"Sounds like you ended up in a good situation, all things considered. How did you end up with the agency? Tell someone's fortune and get it right?" The two shared a hushed snicker, keeping tactical silence.

"No, no crystal ball here. I was in the agency as a paper pusher. One day I opened my big mouth when my supervisor made some disparaging comments about mystics and such. Without going into too much detail, my intuitions were all spot on and I landed in, what's that you called it? A dream job?"

"And if you tell me more about it, you'd have to kill me?"

"Nah, but it is classified. What I can tell you, since you're so curious, is that I have made a few really impressive predictions," Gus started with a bit of a pause.

"Go on then …" Citalli urged him to continue.

Searching his memory for some unclassified but prominent events that Citalli may have heard about, Gus placed his thumb and forefinger on the tip of his chin. "Just last year I predicted the eruption of Mount Nyiragongo in the Congo. I also predicted the Passover Massacre in Netanya, Israel."

"Wait," Citalli started, "if you predicted them, why were so many people still harmed? I mean, I get it, you couldn't stop the volcano. That doesn't stop you from moving the people. And as for the massacre, why not prevent it all together?"

"That, my friend, is exactly why we're here!" Gus stated with an enthusiastic whisper, keeping noise discipline intact. "My superiors were less than convinced that I was the real deal. In short, they didn't act because they didn't believe."

"I see, when you had visions of a catastrophic weapon so close to U.S. soil, they had to step up," Citalli replied in a matter-of-fact fashion.

"And there it is. In a nutshell, yes, they couldn't risk sitting idly by again. Not to put too fine a point on it, Citalli, that's exactly how you got here!"

The two went on talking for hours. They covered everything from sports to fast cars. It really seemed as though a kinship was forming between the two. Maybe someday in the not so distant future, there would be an opportunity for the two to become friends.

"Looks like sunrise is right around the corner," Speaking now to Ramirez and Garcia. "Keep your eyes peeled, you two."

"Got it, Hamilton," Ramirez replied. "All clear at the moment, but we are ready to engage."

True to Agent Hamilton's word, as the sun was rising two men appeared from the southeast corner of the ruins. Moving stealthily, they were dressed in simple attire: black pants, black shoes and, of course, black hoodies.

"I've got two approaching from the southeast. Looks like they have bad intentions. On the brighter side of the news," Ramirez said jokingly, "one's armed with a baseball bat and the other appears to have a lead pipe or something."

"OK, just like we rehearsed. Radio silence until their close enough to apprehend. Try to keep them from damaging the structure."

The two men approached the observatory, hunched over low and moving quickly. Ramirez and Garcia were prepared to use non-lethal means as agreed, tasers only. They positioned themselves in the doorway, Ramirez to the front and Garcia directly behind.

As the two men drew closer, pulse and breathing became more and more rapid. Ramirez raised his left hand just slightly over his shoulder, giving the command to stand by. The two thieves knelt a mere six feet from the structure as the first motioned to his partner with the lead pipe. Clearly the lead pipe would be used in an attempt to penetrate the stone walls of the observatory. He rushed the structure with pipe in both hands, swinging back in a wide arc, then, boom! Ramirez depressed the fire button on his taser. The bolt which emitted was a conductive wire that hit its unsuspecting target like chained lightning.

As the man hit the ground in a convulsing heap of muscle and bone, Garcia exited the door from behind his partner. He pounced on the second unsuspecting man with the stealth of a tiger. He pinned the man to the ground and shoved the taser in his face. "*No te muevas* (Don't move)!" He shouted at the frightened man. He then jerked the man up on his knees, crossed the man's feet behind him and continued to place the man's hands behind his own head.

"Shit, I don't have a pulse," Ramirez shouted as Gus and Citalli exited their doorway.

"On it!" Combat lifesaver skills, good old army training, had prepared Citalli for this situation.

As Garcia glanced over to check on the situation, his unrestrained suspect stealthily grabbed his baseball bat. In an instant he was headed for Citalli, gripping the bat with two hands slugger style, and striking at the back of Citalli's head. Garcia, swung his taser around, letting loose a charged conductive wire.

Like an earthquake exploding from the skies, something powerful consumed the air from around them, twisting reality. A soundless reverberation shook ground and air alike. A radiant ball of light burst amongst the group of men, blinding them. And then, as swiftly as it splintered the skies, the cold and dark of unconsciousness overtook them.

CHAPTER 10

CITALLI WAS AWAKENED BY HIS MOTHER'S VOICE, "MIJO, WAKE UP. Mijo." The voice was distant and muttered, seemingly creeping closer, then closer still. He sluggishly opened his eyes, slowly gaining focus.

Citalli recognized this place. This was where, entranced, he met his mother in prayer. It was a small, square room colored the whitest white, as if the room were built from the clouds themselves. The four walls, the floor, the ceiling, all was consumed by a translucent white void. But why was he here? He had not begun to pray. Was he dead? Was that light truly the weapon Gustavo thought it was.

"Mother? What ... what happened? Why am I here?"

Citalli was still trying to shake the cobwebs out. The last couple of moments of cognitive memory were scrambled. He could remember attempting CPR, or at least kneeling by the victim before the lights went out.

"You're ok, mijo, you're just fine. Don't worry, you're not dead, although you did take quite a blow. Tell me now, what do you remember?"

"I remember there was a man, when we subdued him, stunned him, he quit breathing. I was going to start CPR. All at once

99

something hit me in the back of the head, but at the same time there was an intense light. After that, I woke up here."

"By all rights, you should be dead, mijo. You were saved by Coquihani, the radiance you saw was of the light god Coquihani. Did you hear me, mijo?"

Trying to shake the dust off and collect his thoughts, he was always amazed at how young his mother appeared in his dreams and prayers. She was about five and a half feet tall, hair the deepest black with eyes such a dark brown they were a shadowy black, gleamingly emitting the luminescence of the most brilliant onyx. Those eyes were slightly sunken in giving her an eternal beauty. Her dark hair rested atop wide shoulders, seemingly wide enough to carry Citalli to this chamber of prayer. Her concerned smile was met by her son through the eyes of a child. Ever his mother's son, he felt all of ten years old when in her presence.

"Did I fail him? I was trying to protect our peoples' legacy," Citalli said nervously. In prayer, Citalli always tried to be mindful and respectful. Jokes were thought to be a little out of sorts here in this place of reverence.

"Fail him? No, mijo, you didn't fail him." She was smiling, glowingly filled with pride. "This was a blessing from Coquihani. You are descended from Cocijo, and though Cocijo still slumbers, you are still of the gods. Coquihani and the other gods have begun divine spells and incantations in preparation for the awakening."

"Awakening? They're going to awaken Cocijo? But, when? A day? A week? A year?"

"When your son, my grandson, is ready." Looking more affectionately now and speaking softly, "That's right mijo, your son is the conduit that will withstand the storm that is to come. Your son, Canneo, descendant of Cocijo."

"So, his name's been chosen for me? What else do I need to do? I mean, are there some rites of passage? Signs I'm supposed to look for?"

"Just be his father, mijo. Teach him of life, of our ways, of the world around him. I know he will have love. By the time Cocijo is ready to awaken, Canneo will be ready."

She grabbed her son by the arm, interlocking hers with his. "Come with me Citalli," she said beginning to walk towards an opening corridor. "Here, now, you will witness what happened. Perhaps you will come to see what events led to Cocijo's decision. Why he began his slumber."

As she walked to the corridor, the walls seemed to brighten as if an invitation to enter had been extended. Absolutely dumbfounded, Citalli wondered if he were in a dream, or actually amongst the clouds in prayer. After all, they had never before journeyed beyond the prayer room.

The corridor seemed endless, as if they could walk it forever, until the corridor ceased to extend and became a large room. The color never changed, truly why the ancient ones must have called themselves the cloud people.

A bench was fashioned from the cloud. His mother extended her hand, "Sit, Citalli, please. I can feel you questioning something, why the confusion? What's bothering you, mijo?"

"It's just, well, I didn't pray to you mother. I'm afraid this is all a dream. You say I'm having a son. You've even named him Canneo. I guess it just all seems like a bit too much."

"The night you were born, I looked to the heavens, searching the stars for a sign, any sign, something to sway my heart from doubt. You know this, you were born under the stars that very night. So, I searched until one star caught my eye and I focused on that star. The star was distant, yet still shined so brightly. In that moment, the pain subsided as I heard you cry, my Citalli, my little star. Little did I know, that star, the star I was drawn to, is known today as Capella. Many years ago, it was known to our people as the home of Coquihani. You see, you are the descendant of Cocijo, blessed by Coquihani. This, my little star, is no dream."

"So, then what are you going to show me? Were there wars in the heavens or among the gods that made Cocijo fall into this sleep?"

"There was no war in the heavens, mijo. All manner of beings, even gods, must rest. Many of the gods were angered by the wrong doings of our people after conquest. The mixing with Spanish and French bloodlines is not thought to be a suitable excuse for the atrocities committed. Our people are killing each other for greed and power. When Cocijo awakens there will be a reckoning. The gods will judge the good, the bad, the worthy. You know this."

"Mother, you taught me that I pray to you, and you to the gods; this is still true?"

"Yes, mijo … of course."

"Now that I have been blessed by Coquihani, will he answer my prayers? Can I now pray to the gods?"

"Nothing changes, Citalli. That was my prayer Coquihani answered when he saved you. When you ascend to the clouds then, and only then, will your prayers be answered by the gods."

"But now, at least I know they see me. There's a difference, mother, between thinking and knowing. I guess I should be careful what I say now, huh?" Feeling calmer now, Citalli is able to laugh a little.

"There's my boy," she said lovingly. "My boy is right there, right there in that smile. Many of our prayers together have been without smile until now. Of course, they watch, they have always watched, no need to change yourself, mijo."

"OK then, I guess I'm ready to see what you've brought me here for. Show me."

Views of an ancient civilization appeared in the distance of the translucent wall in front of them. They drew ever closer until they were near, then closer still until Citalli stood amongst them, engulfed by the city. He jolted in a sudden panic, he was surrounded by people, walking with them! Taking his hand, his mother said calmly, "We only appear to be with them, but this is a vision. They cannot see or touch us, this is in the past. Do you understand? We have nothing to fear, we cannot touch or change the past."

Reaching out and passing his hands through a passing elderly man, Citalli confirmed his hand would pass through the figures before him. "It's just so real," he said. Then, recomposing himself through a few deep breaths, "Sorry, mother. Please, keep going."

"This city is Lyobaa, do you remember I told you of it?"

"Yes, today it is known as Mitla. Still revered by our people to this day."

"Yes, it is Mitla. For centuries our people dominated the Oaxaca. We conquered through warfare and through diplomacy. Diplomacy was preferred, it is difficult to build an empire without a human workforce. Our elders believed divinity was passed to them only through elite bloodlines; nothing could be further from the truth. All of our people are descended from the gods, from beyond the clouds. You know of these gods: Cocijo, god of lightning and rain; Coquihani, god of light; Copijcha, god of war; Cozobi, God of maize; Pecala, god of dreams. We, the cloud people, are descended from them. We are allowed entry to and through the clouds not just because of our ancestry, but because of our deeds. Not only mighty warriors, but loyal servants to the gods as well. What we do means something, Citalli. We built great empires to appease the gods; we killed in their name, but why? Can you tell me?"

"We conquered for greatness. Not our greatness, but theirs. We honored them with blood rituals and offerings." Citalli knew the early teachings, and the teachings seemed to be all true, even the very notion that his mother would reside in the clouds.

"We conquered in an attempt to join our people, all of our people. We sacrificed the weak in an attempt to thin out the unworthy. These were judgments we were not meant to make. We were never divine! We were descended from divinity as imperfect, all of us, mijo."

"Do you see now, Citalli? Our thirst for blood was not given to us from the gods. Our blood is returned to the earth to replenish the earth. Our battles were meant to unite us as one people. That's how you honor the gods, through unity. Somehow, we lost our way. The gods grew weary as we drifted further from our purpose, as we misread their wishes and destroyed one another for earthly possessions and power. Cocijo went to Pecala distraught, exhausted, and disillusioned. Pecala induced a great sleep and dream for the weary Cocijo. With Cocijo slumbering, Copijcha would not commit to the war of the Aztec or of the Spaniards."

"So, they just let us lose? They watched as we were enslaved and murdered? Make me understand," Citalli was in tears as he watched the decades come and go through the visions surrounding him. He watched a once mighty civilization wither and decay.

"Men make wars, not gods. Should Copijcha decide to intervene, then he may do so, but men must earn his favor through their actions and their bravery. If gods won wars, why would men bother to fight them? If an army has earned Copijcha's favor, he may grant it. With Cocijo in one of Pecala's dream worlds, Copijcha's blessings would not be granted."

"So, mother, you're saying that our ancestors failed the gods? What happened to free will? What happened to freedom?"

"Freedom? Listen to me son, I'm going to tell you all you need to know about freedom. Freedom isn't free! It never was, and it never will be. Your society believes that freedom has been won, but nothing could be further from the truth! You believe you have freedom of speech, but all speech is judged, every word, every time. So, I ask you, is it really free?"

"Well, now that you put it like that, no. I guess it isn't. But does that apply to all freedoms? How about freedom of religion? One of the biggest reasons our family immigrated to the United States was freedom of religion, so we could practice our beliefs."

"Can Hindu women practice suttee? How about the Santeria and kosher slaughter? Bloodletting? Sacrifice? OK, maybe those are too violent for modern civilizations such as you are accustomed to. May a Mormon man have more than one bride?"

"So, the lesson is what? Controlling my own destiny only goes so far. As much as I am in control, I am not."

"Perfection is an unachievable goal. Control is a dream. Choice is always available! We don't always make the correct choice, we don't always have time to make those choices. Our choices do, however, impact the world around us."

"OK, ok, I understand, really I do." Puzzling though, Citalli thought, with so many people striving for perfection, how have we fallen so far? Not Mexico, not the United States, but the entire world seems lost. Demanding freedoms while offering nothing in return. Something for nothing, the modern interpretation for providence.

"Back to our stroll through history, huh? Again, we are in Lyobaa some five hundred years ago. King Ahuizotl of the Aztec and King Cosijoeza of the Zapotec have engaged their people in a years long war. The fiercest civilizations in our world battled day after day, week after week. Who were the gods to intercede when man challenges man? Since the first man drew his first breath, a battle for survival began. The Aztec clearly had the upper hand, watch."

As Citalli watched, a spectator to war, blood flowed like clotting rivers. Men, women, and children were killed as the blood lust grew out of control. Mothers grabbed obsidian blades to protect their children. None were shown mercy and the city was lost.

Facing a structure that has long since been covered, Citalli sees a man charging from an antechamber and into the courtyard. The man was covered in orange and white paint, apart from the skin around his eyes which was covered in black paint. He wore a vest of ocelot fur and was armed with a spear. Ferocious and profoundly savage, the man defended an underground temple. All movement froze as if someone had paused a video.

"What do you see, Citalli?" His mother asked.

"This man, he looks more like a priest than a warrior. He's not giving up, he's so, so, I don't know, brave."

"Lyobaa was the religious capital of our people. The Aztec believe that they can destroy the gods by destroying the temples of the gods. They were wrong. In a final show of strength and, perhaps against the will of his fellow gods, Coquihani intervenes in a show of respect for the great priest. Watch carefully."

Again, the battle commenced. As the priest defended his keep, an Aztec warrior lunged at him from behind with a macuahuitl. This primitive and effective weapon of war resembled a large wooden paddle with razor sharp obsidian blades embedded along its cutting edges. Gleaming, thirsty obsidian edges slicing through the air eager to taste flesh.

As if from a memory or a dream a ball of light appeared, soundless reverberation shook the ground and consumed the air. A radiant ball of light burst amongst them. Coquihani rescued the priest in the same manner as he had Citalli. So, Citalli thought to himself, the gods are capable of earthly intervention!

"Look familiar, mijo? Only the most selfless devotion to the gods warrants this. Coquihani's actions sent a clear message to the Aztec warriors, who would never again set foot on Zapotec lands. Coquihani's actions would halt the bloodshed until the arrival of the Spaniards two decades later."

"And with the greatest warriors of both kingdoms either dead or wounded, our people were vulnerable to the invading force?" Citalli deduced.

"Vulnerability that affected them when fighting other men, yes. These vulnerabilities would also affect them while fighting the European diseases which were brought to our lands by these invaders."

The city of blood, turmoil and ritual along with its decimated population evaporated around him. The clouded translucence of the previous room was returned.

"How come all I see is a ball of light? Doesn't Coquihani have a form?" Having seen the ball of light twice now, Citalli was curious as to what the god of light really looked like.

"He is a divine spirit, mijo. He appears as he chooses to appear."

"And you, mother? Do I see your spirit?"

"What you see of me now is a projected image in your prayer, an image I project to you."

"And as a spirit, you can see that Kara and I are having a boy? How long have you known?"

"I know because she gave birth as you ascended here, mijo. Would you like to see?"

"No! When I see my son, I want to see him with my own eyes. I want to hold him. I want to protect him."

"Of course, you do, mijo. I know you're going to be a great father. But I must ask you please, try not to be bitter when you wake, you may not view everything as a blessing, but everything that has happened, all of it, it's all for a reason."

"What do you mean?" A flush of heat pulsed through Citalli's face, immediately followed by a shooting chill of arctic cold in his spine. What was she keeping from him?

Slowly forming a warm smile, she cupped her palm around Citalli's cheek. Her eyes began to glass over as she leaned forward to kiss him on the forehead.

"Fine, you're just fine. You were taken to Hospital Reforma in Oaxaca. You did take a baseball bat to the head, after all. You're going to be just fine mijo, after surgery."

"Surgery? How is that fine? How am I supposed to raise a son if …"

"Stop, mijo! I told you, you're fine!" Scolding Citalli seemed the only way to calm him down. Maybe it would have been best had she not told him about the surgery or the hospital.

"Look," she paused for a moment to lift his chin, "do you think Coquihani saved your life to let you suffer?"

Taking deep, controlled breaths and trying to compose himself, Citalli Removed her hand from his chin and held it softly. "I'm sorry. I just have to know, I have to. How bad was I hurt?"

"I believe the doctor used the term 'brick wall' when he talked about your head," she said, smiling to calm his nerves. "Two vertebrae in your neck were damaged and have been repaired. When you wake, you can ask the doctor exactly what he found and fixed. What he said to your friends was that you would be just fine after some rest. Now, stop worrying."

"My friends?" Citalli had completely forgotten about the mission. "Is everyone ok? How about the thieves? Details!"

"Everyone is just fine, mijo. Your friend, Gustavo, stayed the night in Oaxaca to make sure you were alright. Now, keep me in your prayers. Until next time …"

The translucent room, along with the image of his mother, began to fade. Her face and her smile grew slowly more and more shadowy until the obscurely vague images dissipated to a blur. His eyes were opening, and there was nothing but pain and incoherent images.

"Citalli, Citalli, can you hear me?" A female voice was speaking to him, the sounds reverberating in his skull like a grenade just detonated.

Fighting to move and shaking off grogginess Citalli muttered, "Yes, I hear you."

"On a scale of one to ten, what is your pain level?" The voice, suffocated by a thick Spanish accent, became more clear. "Stay with me, one to ten?"

Lungs now on fire, filling with air as they expanded and contracted. "Ten, no eleven," a growl and a grimacing attempt at a smile.

The nurse proceeded to inject morphine into Citalli's intravenous drip. "OK, relax now, just relax." Citalli was fighting the medication in an attempt to remain awake, but the drug relentlessly sped its way into and though his bloodstream. As quickly as he had regained his consciousness, it was gone.

CHAPTER 11

EYES CRUSTED OVER WITH DRIED MUCUS, FEELING THE NUMBING pain of fresh surgical wounds sutured together in his neck, Citalli finally came to. As his eyes peered open through a gritty web engulfing his eyelids, he inhaled and exhaled deeply. Breathing in through his nose and out through his mouth. *Who poured desert sand in his mouth and freeze dried his lips?!*

Seated in the chair beside him, smiling like a child admiring a mud puddle, was Gus. "Hey buddy, I thought we lost you there for a while. Ha ha! Would you like some ice chips? Doc says you can't have water just yet, so ice chips will have to do!"

Mouth parched and throat dry, Citalli managed to squeak out a "Yes." Gus, knowing Citalli would wake at any minute, already had a cup of ice chips ready. How efficient.

"Nice and slow now," Gus moved slowly and raised the top half of the hospital bed just a tad. "That better? Up more? Down?"

As Citalli felt the freezing ice chips teasing his senses back to something resembling normal, he placed his thumb and forefinger together and gave Gus the OK sign. He then moved his hand to the center of his chest as if pondering how much speech may hurt. Clearing his throat with a grunt, "How long have I been here?"

"I'd say about eight hours, just a guess. Hold on … Nurse!" Gus yelled into the hallway, prompting the nurse's smiling face to appear in the doorway.

"Señor Patee, you're awake!" The nurse was an extremely short woman not even reaching the five-foot threshold. She looked like an angel with her hair pulled back into what could have been a pony tail, only a tad shorter. She had a dark complexion, neatly plucked eyebrows, and her face glowed with a natural beauty that required zero makeup. "Let me get the doctor, wait here."

Citalli laughed and coughed, "Where the heck am I going to go?" Looking at Gus who was already hilariously laughing and holding his side. "Oh, dude, laughing hurts. Stop." He was still holding his chest like that had a chance of holding back the laughter, or the pain for that matter.

"You're the one with jokes, knucklehead! Oh man, the look on your face was priceless. Ha ha, quit looking at me like that or I won't be able to stop."

What little hair Citalli had looked like it was glued into place so as to resemble tidal wave. His lips were still so dry that it gave his mouth a snarled look as he attempted to smile. Not to mention his eyes were still bloodshot from the pain meds.

An old, frail looking Caucasian man entered the room. He looked as if he last took a nibble off a sandwich about two weeks ago. He had neatly trimmed hair on head and face, must've spent hours getting that beard right. This signaled a technician in every sense of the word. He simply had to be the surgeon.

"Mister Patee," he opened with a poor attempt at a smile, "how do you feel?"

"You're American!" Citalli seemed surprised an American physician would prefer the scenery in this arid climate, not to mention the non-stop violence.

"Yes. I am from Chicago, that makes the crime here seem almost normal, almost. Now, how do you feel?"

"Besides the obvious tiredness? I guess this feeling of severe dehydration is halfway normal, huh? Anyway, I have numbness and pain in the back of my head and neck. It's not severe, but it does hurt."

"That sounds pretty normal for a man in your condition. Deep breaths in and out, nice and steady." The Doctor placed a stethoscope on Citalli's chest and listened to his breathing. Then centered the stethoscope over the center of the chest, "just breathe normally now." He then proceeded to check the eyes and ears, along with a quick test for feeling in Citalli's hands and feet.

"You took quite a blow to the head and neck, young man! Oh, so sorry. Where are my manners? My uh, my name is Doctor Sutherford." The man registered about a zero on the charisma scale if there was such a thing. "Just a few ice chips for the time being, I will be back in an hour or so, then we'll talk. Nurse Santiago will take care of you until then, just press the red button there." He pointed at the pager device placed by Citalli's hand with the red call button on it.

"Got it, thanks. I really don't know what else to say, just, thank you!"

"You're quite welcome sir, it's what we do here." Another attempted smile accompanied by a wink and off he went.

"Gussy, Gus! Gustavo! I expect this other button is for my morphine, huh?" Citalli sounded like maybe he didn't need anymore.

"Should he have anymore?" Gus motioned at Nurse Santiago.

"It's ok," she said, "Less pain, better blood pressure. Besides, it will only allow him the prescribed amount." Smiling and giggling, "Señor, can I get you anything else? Another pillow or blanket?"

"Ice! Please, more ice. I'm so dry." Not that he was trying to play the sympathy card, but surgery just has a way of sucking the life right out of you. Funny, he thought, how something so physically draining could save your life.

She nodded and proceeded to get the ice. Handing the cup to Gus, she dunked her hand in a waving motion as if placing him in charge of ice detail. A flirtatious nod from Gus and she was on her way.

Citalli waited for the nurse to exit the room, then hit Gus with a couple of questions that demanded answers.

"Did everyone make it out ok? Oh, and that includes me. What do you know about my condition?"

"Everyone's great, and yes, even you. They expect a full recovery, though I'm not sure what the army's medical review board's going to say about that neck injury; it's a little difficult to predict at this point. All the same, Doctor Sutherford insists you'll have full range of motion. As for Garcia and Ramirez, I sent them home on a commercial flight. We thought it best, all things considered, if they made their way back to the United States."

"Best I could hope for all things considered, I guess. Thank you for being here when I woke up, it kinda kept me from freaking out." The two shared a still weak handshake.

"Next questions Gus: did we complete the mission? Any damage to the site?"

"The local police on site apprehended both perps; turns out our back-up was far enough away to remain conscious. Anyway, they cuffed the two thieves while everyone was still knocked out, so I guess that's a yes so far as success is concerned. There's been no evidence of any type of ancient weapon, besides of course, the flash of light that seemingly knocked us all unconscious. How much of that do you remember?"

"Well, I remember attempting to give CPR, a bright light moving in as I was getting bashed in the head, then lights out."

"Yeah, that's pretty much where we're at. There's no explanation for the orb of light. It was so bright that it fried every camera in the security system. I suppose that would make my premonition correct, just maybe misinterpreted a little. At least that's my guess. We swept the entire area for radiation, everything checked out. Everyone on site was briefed to remain silent; so naturally, it's all over the news." The two shared a chuckle.

"Dude, what did I say about making me laugh?" Citalli paused to regain composure a little, "Anyway, have you called Kara?"

"Shouldn't that have been your first question?"

"Hey, I'm on drugs," Citalli smiled, "prescription drugs, legal baby!"

"OK goofus, I'll let you get away with it, then. The answer is yes, Kara gave birth right about the time you were getting knocked out apparently."

"A boy!" Citalli interjected.

"Yeah, and how did you know? You the clairvoyant now?"

"I just know. Maybe someday I'll tell you, but I just know. I'm the dad, remember?"

Gus Grinned in amusement. *Lucky guess*, he thought. "They said he looks just like his father, then they said he was handsome. I was like, ok, now I'm confused."

Citalli laughed so hard he nearly choked on a chunk of ice. "What a guy! I'm laying here half drugged up and in agony, and you can't accept the fact that I'm sexy! I mean look at this gown, bro?"

"Very sexy, Señor!" The nurse giggled as she walked by. "You should see your hair!"

"If a man looks sexy with bed head, that's a good-looking man! My wife will be ecstatic when I get home," Citalli said. He then turned back to Gus, "You know what to do!"

"OK, ok. Before we call Kara, there's one more thing. About the mission, of course. When we came to, you were bleeding pretty good. The locals smartly called for medical help, you know, an ambulance." Gus paused for a moment and gathered his emotions together. "Anyway, I applied a field dressing to your wound and applied a little bit of pressure while we waited."

"I knew you had my back Gus. Thank you," Citalli said looking down suppress anything unhappy. He would not let anything spoil the upcoming conversation with Kara.

"I did have your back, I still do. It's just, they told Kara and family that I saved your life. Look, all I did was place the bandage and hold pressure. I did what anyone else would have done, given the situation."

"No, Gus, that isn't true. Of all the people that were there, only you thought to apply first aid; just you! So, while anyone could have done it, they didn't. Again, thank you. I'll never forget it."

Felling a little more at ease now, Gus picked up the phone beside the bed. He pulled the phone number from a crumpled piece of paper in his pocket, then dialed.

"Mrs. Patee's room please, her husband would like to have a word." Gus, with a silly giving gesture and bow, handed the phone to Citalli.

"Citalli, babe, are you alright?" Kara's voice was trembling with concern.

"I'm fine girly-girl," Citalli said softly, with a lump the size of Manhattan in his throat. "How are you and our new addition doing?"

"They told you?" She had wanted to surprise him.

"No, I just knew. I'll explain later," Citalli said, not wanting to divulge his conversation with his mother in present company. They may get the idea he was hallucinating. After all, the old ways were all but lost; not to mention he suffered a head injury mere hours ago.

"Then you'll be happy to know I have honored our arrangement. Do you remember, babe?"

"Yes," Citalli said. "You would name a girl and I would name a boy. His name is Canneo, C-a-n-n-e-o. No middle name."

Giggling through the muffled phone call she said, "Hey, I never said it was a boy."

"I know you didn't, but I knew that too." Then shifting his accent to that of a pirate, "I felt it in me bones!"

Kara laughed hysterically, "I guess you ARE ok. Same silly Citalli. I love you, babe."

"I love you too, girl." Glancing up, "Oh-oh, looks like my doctor found his way back to my room. I'll call you back later, ok?"

The two exchanged a goodbye and an audible click ended the moment of blissful reunion. Clearing his throat with a cough and a fist thumping his chest, Citalli turned to face Doctor Sutherford. No words, just an attentive glance shot in the doctor's direction.

Like reading a script, the doctor fumbled through and read from Citalli's file, as if anyone could truly read physician scribbling. Then, slightly tilting his head up and looking through the gap above his glasses said, "You're a lucky man Mister Patee. There appears to be no damage to your skull, though two of your cervical vertebrae were damaged. The appropriate technique, we determined, was to fuse the C3, C4, and C5 vertebrae together. This procedure was accomplished with what appears to be no complications."

"So, doc, give it to me straight. Fused vertebrae, I get that, but what exactly does that mean, short and long term?" Citalli had a son to raise, and a wife to support.

"I see no reason why you shouldn't make a complete recovery, minus some general discomfort. Modern anti-inflammatory medications should relieve most of that. Some physical therapy will undoubtedly be necessary, but that's nothing that can't be taken care of back home."

The doctor placed Citalli's patient record down and continued, "You should be cleared for discharge from the hospital the day after tomorrow, barring any unforeseen circumstances. We'll just need to observe you overnight to ensure there are no further issues. If you're feeling better, and you *should* be feeling better, we'll remove the morphine drip tomorrow. We'll observe you for one more day, this time without intravenous pain medications. If you've shown the expected progress, you'll be free to go. Any other questions?"

"No, I guess the rest of my questions will be answered by army doctors when I get back." He turned his attention to Gus, "What if this ends my career, Gus? What about my family?"

"Try not to think about that right now," Gus replied in a soft tone. "You're a soldier. You were on an official mission for the United States Government. If this impacts your ability to serve, I'm sure the Veterans Administration will take care of you. I'm going to personally see to it that you're well taken care of. This mission was classified but official, got it? Remember, I've got your back."

"We'll wait and see, I guess," Citalli said unconvincingly. "Now," he said, pressing the button for more morphine, "I'm going to knock out for a while."

CHAPTER 12

U PON BEING RELEASED FROM THE HOSPITAL, GUS AND CITALLI once again boarded the jet and headed home. Still tired from the past couple of days, the only sounds in the cabin of the craft were that of two men snoring. Dreams of little Canneo danced through the heart and mind of Citalli. Career or not, he knew he had a more important job in front of him: fatherhood.

After a short briefing from his commanding general and a quick check up at the hospital, Citalli was released on convalescent leave while he recovered from his surgery. Gus finally got to drive that roadrunner as he chauffeured Citalli home, but not before he got an earful about what would happen to him should a scratch find its way onto that machine.

"Are you sure you don't need to stop and take a moment before we get to your house?" Gus wanted to make sure Citalli was emotionally ready to see Kara and Canneo. "Really, it's not a problem."

"I'm sure. I need this like you would not believe, and the sooner the better! I mean, don't get me wrong, I love my wife like nothing else in this world. So don't get the impression that I didn't need her before, I did. Right now though, I, I just need to see her face. Funny,

I only really feel complete when she's there; even if she's right down the road at her mom's, I miss her. Wimpy, huh?"

"Not at all," began Gus, "I often wish I had someone like that. You're a lucky man: lucky to be alive, and lucky to have the gift of family. I guess I'm lucky you're alive too. I got the impression Kara would hunt me down if I didn't bring you back!"

Grinning now from ear to ear Citalli said, "Yup! You're one lucky dude! But listen, if you're looking for love, I can introduce you to some really nice ladies; really Gus, it's not a problem. Everybody has needs, and you seem like you could use some love in your life, nothing personal."

"Thanks, but no," Gus declined. "I know it sounds a little cliché, but I'm in love with my work. Can you imagine if I fell in love, then had some kind of premonition about her death? That would destroy me! I'm actually a little more sentimental than you think. It's just that I see these things, sometimes beautiful, sometimes horrible; I have to try to remain detached. No gift is without at least a fraction of curse. Trust me on this one Citalli, no strings no problems."

"OK, no pressure. But listen, you're a well-educated man and quite the catch, don't forget that. While we're on the subject of education, Kara and I will be home schooling Canneo, and you could always sign up for substitute duty." Citalli was laughing but very serious. "Honestly," he continued, "I feel like I've known you a lifetime, you're family now."

"Well, thank you Citalli. That means a bunch, really it does. Maybe I'll drop in from time to time and check on little Canneo." As if the dream began where the journey ended, they were home. "Ready Citalli?"

Citalli reached his arm out and placed his hand on Gus's shoulder. He drew his breath a few times, and then, rolling his shoulders forward, "OK, I'm ready, let's do this!"

The vehicle came to a stop as Citalli began to open the car door, he spotted Kara coming out of the front door. It seemed as if the car door willed itself open as he floated blissfully on air and gracefully into the loving embrace he longed for. He pulled her close and frantically searched for words, "Shhhh, not yet, don't say a thing," he whispered in her ear. Nothing in heaven or on earth could replace the pure joy in this moment. This was but a heartbeat, a moment in time. He pulled back just enough to plant a kiss or three on her cheek which was salty and sweet from teardrops.

"Miss me?" A smile planted itself firmly onto his face. "Did you miss me?" He asked again.

"When they called and said you were hurt … what would I do without you?" The tears gushed and poured.

He grabbed her and held her again, "Easy baby, I'm home now. I'm home."

Gus was motionless. Standing no more than ten feet away, he felt consumed by emotion. He stared down at his own shadow trying to get a hold on the moment and trying to fight back his own tears. Protocol dictated he remain as emotionless as a blade of grass. He reminded himself that crying wouldn't exactly meet that protocol (silly man). He suppressed the urge as if to exude some false sense of strength.

As the lovers' embrace concluded Kara turned her attention to Gus and slowly walked to him. She reached out her right hand and grabbed his left elbow, "Thank you Gus. Thank you so much for bringing him home." She could barely see his face as she continued to wipe the tears from her own.

"A promise is a promise," he said softly, "and I'm a man of my word."

"Yes, you are, and there's someone inside waiting to meet the two of you," Kara said, rediscovering a firm and happy speaking tone and glowing with pride. "Canneo was just starting to wake up when you pulled in. I guess he already knows Daddy's here."

"Yeah, well he better! You know who the man is around here!" Laughter broke out between them.

"That must be the pain meds kicking in again," Gus said.

"No, it not the meds. We've got it down to a science," Kara said. "He's the man. I'm the boss."

They made their way into the house, and there, in his grandmother's arms, lie the true miracle of life. "Don't be shy, Citalli. Come and say hello," Canneo's grandmother said.

"Thank you, Mirabelle," Citalli said as he gently reached to hold his newborn son. "Canneo, no doubt named for the rivers running from my own eyes. You even smell like the birth of water itself. Water is life as you are my life now, son. I promise, as long I live, I will be here for you."

Funny how soon babies seem to be attentive. Young Canneo stared into his fathers' eyes as if there was no one else in the room. He was a good-sized boy, twenty-inches long and eight pounds. Beautiful pale bronze skin with brown eyes seemingly sculpted from the deepest darkest mahogany.

"Look at all that hair!" Gus said. "He's perfect, Citalli, just perfect!"

"And you two must be perfectly hungry! Plenty of people have brought food by, there's loads to eat in the kitchen. Give me the baby and get something to eat, huh?" Grandma was giving instructions and eager to hold little Canneo again.

The group made their way into the kitchen where all kinds of meat and side dishes waited in neat little trays for them. There were signs, ribbons, and cards congratulating the family on the birth of Canneo. Citalli and Gus, thinking alike, went straight for the cake.

"Citalli," Kara said, "I want to ask you something, right here in front of Gus."

"Uh-oh, this doesn't sound good," Gus nervously added.

"I'm all ears girly-girl," Citalli said. "This should be good," he said, laughing menacingly.

"I was wondering, Gus, you seem like such a good man. Besides the fact that you got my husband into all kinds of trouble, you did save his life! When he was in the hospital, you stayed with him," pointing to her husband. "Somehow, your secret little mission added even more meaning to the word family. Citalli is still here because of you, because you cared. So, the question is: Citalli, can Gustavo here be godfather to little Canneo? He did save your life, after all."

Citalli was taken aback a bit and noticed Gus was blushing, clearly blindsided by the question. "I think that would be awesome! So, what do you say Gus? You, uh, kinda have to volunteer."

"Well, that's the sort of thing a person doesn't say no to, isn't it? Of course, I will. One demand though, I want a phone call every year on his birthday," Gus said.

"No problemo! You got it! Now, eat you two," Kara said as she turned her attention to the living room and little Canneo.

"When are you headed back to DC?" Citalli was kind of wondering if the two men would be able to share a little male bonding time together.

"I'm supposed to fly out around noon tomorrow. With any luck, Garcia and Ramirez have most of the paperwork nailed down by then. Why? What's up?" He asked.

"How about you spend the night again tonight? I have a few thoughts I'd like to share with you, and maybe I could provide you with some explanations to a few things."

Gus, staring down at the plate, thought there might be something else rattling around in that freshly popped melon of his. "Sure! That would be great. But, no beer this time, you're on medication."

"Great!" Citalli said smiling, "Now, if you're done guarding that plate, let's go for a walk."

Citalli informed Kara of their intentions and out the door they went. Back down the path and to the pond. Citalli used the pond as sort of a pool of reflection. It was easier to think when staring into the murky waters. Something about water always seemed so soothing. A duck paddled through the water without a care in the world. Not fishing, not bathing, just majestically gliding across the stillness of the pond as if seeking attention.

"I like it out here," Citalli started. "This is where I come to think. Sometimes I come here so I don't have to think. I can stand on the banks of this pond and look at the water for hours. I can see if the scarecrow in my cornfield is doing his job, not to mention see if the corn is growing."

"It certainly is peaceful. That evening sun's hot, but somehow, it's heat on my face is therapeutic." Gus seemed to be in agreement with Citalli. "Is there something on your mind?"

"There is, Gus. To be honest, I'm almost apprehensive to tell you, but with your gift of foresight I figure you might be able to wrap your head around it. I'm going to tell you what happened if, and only if, you promise me it stays here between us. Also, you have to keep an open mind. This is not the medicine talking. Sound like a bargain you're willing to make?"

"Since I'm now the godfather of your child, if you have answers, you better tell me what happened," Gus joked and let out a laugh. "But seriously, I'd really like to hear what you've got to say. I promise, it stays here as if you were speaking to the water."

"You said you visited Monte Albàn as a tourist. So, you studied our people, maybe studied our religion a little?" Citalli was setting a base for the conversation.

Gus started as if reading from a book, "Prior to the arrival of the conquistadors, the Zapotec people practiced a polytheistic religion, meaning they had multiple gods. My understanding was that there were major and minor gods. The Zapotec called themselves the cloud people. The elite in society were believed to be of divine lineage from the gods, and only the elites were the cloud people. Oh, and though they had gods, they did not pray to them; they prayed to their ancestors, who in turn conversed with the gods for them. Sound about right?"

"Whoa, you really did do some studying! See, you really should consider helping us with Canneo's education." Citalli wasn't joking, that was as accurate a depiction as he'd heard from someone not of Zapotec bloodlines. "Anyway, that's the general gist of it. The elites believed only their ancestors answered prayers from the clouds, they were somehow special. That was never true, but if a commoner claimed otherwise, it could be fatal. The kingdom was run through fear along with the demand for respect for the elites, the descendants of the gods. We are, however, all descended from the gods, all of us. We are all the cloud people. With me so far?"

"You've got my attention. I've spent many years studying various Mesoamerican cultures. There's so much information, but there's also so much information we're missing. The Spaniards' penchant for destruction led to so much erasure of anything not resembling Catholicism, that history was massacred along with the people." Maybe Gus was an expert, of sorts.

"Again, spot on Gus, Canneo's going to have a godfather who understands him. We actually do pray to our ancestors, to this very day. This prayer places us in, well, it's almost a trance. We do not see, nor do we speak with the gods. Let's have a seat, huh?"

The two of them sat along the edge of the pond after a quick look for any critters, especially snakes, in the area.

"I pray to my mother. Not all ancestors answer, and I'm not sure how all of that works. I'm just a man, after all."

"Wait." Gus said in near disbelief, "You actually converse with your mother in prayer?"

"Yes. Well, the spirit of my mother. Anyway, about the ball of light. When that ball of light knocked us out, I was transported to the prayer realm. That's the only time its ever happened to me outside of a prayer."

"Well, maybe it's got something to do with consciousness. Not insinuating that it was a dream, but you were unconscious," Gus added.

"I was knocked out alright, but that's not what got me there. Among our gods, the one I am descended from is called Cocijo."

"God of lightning and rain, right?!" Gus jumped in.

"Yeah, that's the one, and the ball of light we witnessed, that was Coquihani, god of light. You see, that's why all you were able to see was intense light. That's why all security was knocked out, and that's why everyone in the near vicinity was also knocked out. What you witnessed, Gus, was a Zapotec god. Coquihani to be exact."

"Assuming I'm inclined to believe you Citalli, I need something more tangible. Why would a god care about us, or about two thieves out to steal something; something they say was just a cache of jade and other precious stones?"

"Gustavo! I'm sorry, Gus. Do you really think it was that simple? For a deity to appear it takes … well, it takes something more than just some good deed or concern for a higher power. That's not how it works!" Citalli paused for a second. "What do you know about the Observatory? Besides the fact it doesn't conform to the other structures?"

"What we think we know about the structure, is that it was built in the likeness of the constellation Auriga. Its shape is an exact replica of that celestial body, and the brightest star in that body is Capella." Gus was smiling now, amazed at his own intellect.

"That's actually true. That brightest star you mentioned, that's the home of Coquihani. That structure was built to honor him; and to observe the heavens, of course. Like I said, our ancestors pray to the gods. My mother was the one who prayed to him, to protect me as I was protecting him. Coquihani was answering her prayer. Not just because she asked, but because we earned it. Yes, he protected me; but he presented himself before all of us. You said yourself that there was no explanation for the light, no residual traces of any type of weapon. Yet, there it was and here we are."

"What else did your mother tell you in this prayer, or this dream?"

"She told me Kara went into labor exactly when that miracle occurred, making two miracles. She told me it was a boy, and she told me what to name him."

His puzzlement turned to clear thought, Gus was starting to believe this just a little. "So, that's how you knew it was a boy? And she named him, huh? Your mother named him from the spirit world? Is that how the naming works?"

"Good question! I'll have to ask her in my next prayer. I just kind of took it on faith. Never really occurred to me that others get their names like that. I didn't, but I suppose it may not be all that uncommon."

"You're right about one thing," Gus cackled, "I wouldn't dare tell anyone about this. They'd have me thrown into a padded room and restrained. I'm still trying to wrap my mind around the fact I might have seen an ancient Zapotec deity. I don't suppose you or your mother could ask for a sign?"

"Wouldn't you call what we got a sign? You were mere feet away from a god. Just don't let it go to your head, huh? You can either choose to believe or not. Remember, I'm just a man, no need to impress me. Anyway, lets head back to the house, I have something I'd like to show you."

"Sounds like this is getting better! Can I ask what it is?" Gus said.

"My mother gave me something that's supposed to be ancient and spiritual. All she told me was that it was somehow entangled with a supernatural event, not really sure what. I was just a kid, so naturally I was wowed by it. To be honest with you, it's my most prized possession. Since you have a gift, and I have an object; I don't know, it just kinda makes sense."

"You want me to touch and see if it sparks the clairvoyant in me, is that what you mean?" Gus said, clarifying Citalli's request.

"Yup! Not going to be a problem is it?"

"Won't know until I see it, let's get on with it."

The two of them stealthily entered the house, just in case little Canneo was sleeping. Citalli threw a hushing signal at Gus, then threw the same signal along with a come on wave at Kara. The little one had fallen asleep in his grandmother's arms, and she was asleep right along with him.

Entering the room and retrieving an item from a personal fireproof safe, Citalli turned to Kara. "Gus here is a clairvoyant, the real deal. Remember this?"

She nodded, half in disbelief and half in excitement. Throwing an inquisitive look at Gus as if to say, "Let's get on with it."

"Mind if I have a seat?" Gus said motioning at the chair. "It helps a lot, especially if it's something as powerful as you think it is."

"Knock yourself out," Citalli said with a grin, "no pun intended!"

Citalli then proceeded to remove something resembling a pendant from the cloth it was wrapped in. He gently folded the cloth and set the pendant atop it, then extended both hands towards Gus. "Here you go my man," he said in a nervously soft tone. "If you're uncomfortable with this, just say the word."

The pendant was of a brownish orange color and well worn. It certainly looked old. Gus cast a glance to examine it apprehensively while Citalli still held it. "Is that hessonite? I'm no expert when it comes to any precious stones or anything, but it sure looks like hessonite."

"Does it matter? I mean, I'm no expert on either. I know that if it belonged to one of the elites, then its either precious or semi-precious, you know the deal. Are there things that throw off your senses?" Citalli was confused as to why Gus didn't just grab the stone and go to work. "Look, it's some sort of amulet or charm, and its fashioned in the shape of a jaguar head. Again, you don't have to do this, it really wouldn't be a problem."

"I was just admiring it. The craftsmanship screams ancient Mesoamerican. It's beautiful, really. OK, so listen; when I grab the stone, just relax and stay quiet until I'm done. Don't worry, any perceived pain isn't physical on my end. There's always a chance I see nothing, but this appears to have a story to tell; call it intuition," Gus said, half smiling and half readying himself.

Looking for a conformational nod from Kara and Citalli, Gus took a deep breath in, blew it out, then gently grasped the hessonite stone. Grasp may be an inadequate term to use, Gus seemed to recoil as the stone demonstratively bit back. Maybe it was in response to the mystical gift Gus's hand surrounded it with. The stone was causing an obvious tremble in Gus's hand as his eyes closed and his wits were enamored with smells and sounds. The darkness slowly subsided with a hazy view, as if looking through a fogged window, Gus could see an entire city alive with excitement!

Gus began to get his footing as he looked around to take in the spectacle surrounding him. This was Monte Albàn, minus a few of the less ancient structures. Its location was evidenced by the shape and glory of the observatory. Fire in the altar and torches crackled, hissed, and seethed. The ancient ones were alive and all around him, portraying the true strength and power of the long-abandoned kingdom.

A large man shouted incantations, which enlivened the crowd. Gus perceived him to be a priest, perhaps even the high priest. A young man wearing similar garb stood before him, fists clenched and hunched over. Gus could sense the stone he currently had in the palm of his hand was also being held by the younger of the two. He felt as if something else lay in the opposite palm though he could not see it.

Gus watched, awe stricken, as the young man's flesh stretched like elastic, beginning a transformation of sorts into another manner of being. The eyes were the first to change, now boasting the blazing golden eyes of a feline. As cheeks became swollen and protruded, the size and power of predatory jaws burst from within his mouth. Whiskers and fur sprouted to cloak the man's body as if covering it with armor whilst transforming him into a beast. A roar and a scream followed by immense fury; the young man had been transformed into a jaguar! *Shapeshifters were myth*, Gus thought, *but so were clairvoyants for that matter.*

As Gus continued to watch in cognizant amazement as the large cat exited the great city. His once priestly garbs, now tattered and torn, were ceremoniously burned in the hungry flames growling from within the altar. The city burst into celebration, chanting but one word: nagual.

The large man conducting this ritual seemed less than surprised, yet more than delighted. He had a look of pride on his face. A deep sort of pride that only comes through affection—affection that only comes through love. He bent over and picked up not one stone, but two. The stone now in Gus's possession and a matching black stone, perhaps made of onyx or some similar type of stone. This was clearly a powerful spectacle, which had imprinted itself on the stone.

Clear vision turned to haze, haze to darkness, darkness back to the light of current reality. Gus reached towards Citalli with the stone and placed it in his hand. "Here," he said nearly out of breath, "I believe this belongs to you."

Kara rushed into the adjoining master bathroom and filled a cup of water. She was almost running when she came back, "Here! Are you ok, Gus? Drink this!"

"Take your time Gus," Citalli added, "relax. Have a drink."

Slamming the entire cup of water, Gus shook his head, "It's ancient alright. What's more, your mother was correct, it does hold significance. If everything you've told me today is true, Citalli, keep that stone safe. I'm a bit unclear whether the stone holds power, but it is important and way more than just a relic."

Gus proceeded to tell the two of his visions of the ancient city, of its peoples' celebration, and of the shapeshifter himself.

"A nagual," Citalli started in amazement, "So they're not just folklore or legend!"

"That's not it," Gus interjected, "That stone is part of a set. I don't know if the two are twins, opposites, or really anything else about them. I only know that there were two stones. The nagual held one in each hand as his transformation began. The other stone was a shiny black stone, onyx struck me as a possibility."

"I know I don't talk like it, but I do read a lot, Gus." Citalli clearly was on to make a point. "A lot of the top scholars believe that the idea of shapeshifting was brought to this continent from European mythology. We can't exactly use your vision as proof to them; but us, we know. We know that notion was not brought here from the invading forces. It's something that's not just within our culture, but it's something that's real. Something that's really real. Wow!"

"Well, speaking of real, I really need a drink!" Said Gus. "Not water, not beer, a drink. Please tell me you have something to stop the rebellion going on in my brain right now."

"That corn ain't all for eating," Citalli said, "You sure you're up for some homemade corn liquor? Made it myself, a little skill I picked up in the backwoods of Florida."

"That's the first thing you said that's made sense all damn day." Gus said, recalling Citalli using that same phrase the day they met. He looked up at Kara, "Sorry about the language, kinda slipped."

"It's warranted," she said, "so I guess I'll let it slide this time. Just do me a favor, drink that stuff outside. And none for you, Citalli, not until you're better."

The two men took off to the back porch, Gus drank quietly while Citalli snuck in a hook or two. Medicine or not, responsible or not, the past few days were filled with as much discovery and revelation as any one mind could handle.

It's hard to know how to feel when fiction becomes fact, and when trying to determine whether any nagual survived the many years of bloodthirsty war and greed filled enslavement.

"You really didn't know about that?" Gus said, thumb pointing back into the house. "What I mean is, thinking a stone is special, well that's one thing; knowing that the stone was used in what we consider as an impossible event, that's, I don't know. Magical, I guess."

Citalli was staring out into the clear darkness of the night, "When you're a kid, adults tell you all kinds of stuff. You believe almost all of it, what you don't believe you pretend to. But that gemstone, it just had the look and feel of something authentic, something beyond palpable. Even though there was no story with it at the time, I just knew it was unique."

The two sat for hours, telling of old myths and legends. Wondering aloud, as if children again, if the stories were true.

PART THREE

CHAPTER 13

Summer 2013
Taugui, Oklahoma

TEN YEARS PASSED, AND CANNEO HAD BECOME A FULL-FLEDGED country boy, but a country boy like no other. Sure, he happily ran around without shoes. He played around in the grass, mud and fields with no regard for critters and snakes. He was a boy, anxious to learn where he fit in the universe, clear nights were spent studying the stars with his father, Citalli. Medically retired from the army, Citalli had all the time he wanted to teach his son the old ways.

He stood about four and a half feet tall and sported a short haircut, which negated his need for any comb or brush. The tan bronze skin draped over his bony body was well decorated with scuffs, scratches, and a newly scabbed over cut on the knee cap. The dark mahogany in his eyes had not faded.

"Canneo!" His mother shouted from inside the house. "Don't you get dirty today! I want you to make a good impression when you meet your godfather. You hear me?"

"OK mom. Since I can't play, can I watch TV for a while? It is my birthday, you know?" *Best to get while the getting is good*, he thought. *Besides, dad was picking up Gus from the airport.* He figured as long as his father had already been gone, he might still have a little time available.

"I guess so. But no coming in the kitchen, I'm cooking."

Not a word! Not a yes or an ok, just the sound of feet beating. As thrilled as the boy was to finally meet the godfather he spoke to on the phone, well, priorities! Click, click, click; looking for something suitable to watch, then he heard it. The unmistakable sound of daddy's car rumbling down the driveway. Another quick click to turn off the TV as if it were never on. Should he be excited or nervous? Should he walk or run to the car? Maybe just wait, right where he was? Yes, that was it! Wait right here!

"I'm surprised he's not out here already." Canneo could hear his father making excuses for him through the window. "I think you'll be surprised at how big he is. Well, tall … He's a skinny little thing." Still that winner smile and laugh, Citalli hadn't changed much and that was a good thing.

They entered the home, looking around for the birthday boy. "Boo!" Canneo popped out of nowhere.

"Hey boy, boo to you too. What kind of welcome is that? Get over here and meet Gus!"

Shyly skulking and smiling the boy moved over. Head ever so slightly tilted and that unmistakable Patee grin on his face, "Hi," he said in a muttered tone.

"Well, hello Canneo. It's nice to finally meet you. Why so shy? We must have talked on the phone three or four times this year, not to mention all the times I called on your birthday. Do I get a hug?" Gus had been rehearsing a little and hoped it didn't show. All the years at the agency keeping his nose to the grindstone left him little time for relationships, at least relationships outside of the close bond he felt with the Patee's. He was also trying to suppress any form of extrasensory perception. Good or bad, Gus just didn't need the drama that came with such visions, not today.

Gus knelt down and Canneo ran at him with a hug. It was playful and exuberant, warm and affectionate, everything a hug from a young boy should be. "My mom's cooking! she said not to bother her, so I waited here. Come on, I hear you like our pond and there's been a kingfisher down there lately; he's huge!"

"Come on," Citalli said with a chuck on the shoulder, "it's a big kingfisher, we've been watching it for a few days now. He was down there this morning."

Canneo grabbed Gus's hand in a firm playful manner, and the three were seemingly sling-shotted out the door. The boy moved with a purpose pulling and jerking and willing Gus's hand and arm forward.

"Look," he said holding his voice to a muffled shout, "a belted kingfisher," Canneo explained.

Blue and white with an impressive beak. A beak that undoubtedly helped earn him the name of belted kingfisher. He was perched on a log, enjoying the spoils of his hunt.

"They dive into the water head first like a missile," Canneo said, making the diving motion with his hand. "That's how they fish, huh dad?"

"They sure do, son. Like a missile!" Citalli and Gus shared a smile of admiration at the boy's obvious study lesson. "Now boy, let's see if that birthday dinner's ready. I see your grandma's car coming, I'd say that's a clear sign. Straight inside and wash your hands, then you can say hello, deal?"

Canneo had a way with the lack of words, a smile and simple nod of the head and the boy was gone.

"He has to wash his hands for grandma?" Gus said looking befuddled.

"Not normally, no. We got him a puppy, so I don't want him to see it until Kara has a chance to get the camera ready."

When they came along the house Kara and Canneo popped out of the door as if intentionally meeting there. Grandma Mirabelle was already walking away from her car trying to hide the little package inside.

"Where's my little birthday boy?" She yelled, looking around as if not seeing him.

"Grandma!" A run, a jump and a hug. His reward? A firm wet kiss on the cheek.

Mirabelle looked up at the other three, "Are we ready?"

"OK, OK," Citalli said, "it's high time they meet."

A joy filled puzzling look crossed Canneo's face as he pondered what was amiss. His mother, handing the camera to Citalli, took hold of his hand and escorted him to Mirabelle's car and opened the passenger door.

There, on the seat, was a little bitty beagle puppy. Orange and white, with very little black. He made a whining sound and was shivering. His tail wagged with a nervous fervor. The young pup moved closer to Canneo, cautiously craving touch and warmth.

"His name's Louie," Kara said. "Remember, Canneo, he's just a baby; please be gentle."

"OK, I will. Come on Louie." Canneo slowly reached into the car and picked up Louie. The dog reached immediately to Canneo's cheek and licked him. Canneo took the young Louie to a suitably soft patch of grass in the yard. Dog and boy lay in the grass playing and snuggling as if nothing else existed. This just had to be the best birthday ever.

"Canneo," Kara said, "put Louie inside the fence your father made in the backyard, please."

"Can I stay in there with him, Mom?" Canneo said, picking up the puppy.

"Just until we eat." Then, looking at her husband. "Citalli, should we bring the food out to the picnic table?"

Citalli thought that sounded like a great idea. While the two youngsters migrated into the fenced area, the adults moved the birthday meal outdoors to the picnic table. Planning ahead, Citalli had placed the table underneath a silver maple tree which would give the table, and Louie's outdoor playpen, shade during the heat of the day.

Mere days earlier Canneo complained to his father about building the fence so close to the tree. Citalli played it off by telling him it would be a garden for plants requiring partial shade. Still, the boy could spend hours tossing the seed pods from the maple as high as he could and watching them float down to the ground while spinning like helicopter blades; something he could now share with Louie.

"You're a smart guy, Gustavo," Citalli said. "Can you tell me what kind of seed pod this is?"

"Looks to be some kind of maple." He looked up at the tree. "Is that a silver maple?"

"You never cease to amaze me," Citalli said "Now you're an expert on trees too?"

Tossing the seed pod high in the air Gus replied with a laugh, "No, not an expert on trees. Like any kid who grew up with these in the neighborhood, I could play with them for hours. A lot of folks don't like them because their typically very messy trees, not to mention their roots find their way inside water pipes."

Kara, setting down a pitcher of sweetened tea put in her two cents. "Maybe the trees were placed here by nature to amuse our children. Amusement leads to entertainment and curiosity, which lead to imagination, and finally to learning."

"Kara used to be a teacher, Gus." Citalli began to explain. "That's what made it such a great idea for us to homeschool Canneo. You know books, especially history books, change so much over the years. They seem to change to appease people's need for self-worth more than just the newest understanding of events. We want our son to be a free thinker, and we don't want a teacher with hidden agendas to affect his learning curve."

"Come on Citalli," Gus started, "do you really think all teachers have hidden agendas? Help me out here Kara."

"OK you two, let me set the record straight. Teaching is an art form of sorts. To be able to take what you know and transfer those understandings to others. The trick when developing young minds is to present the information and to let them try to determine their own understanding. While all of this is taking place, you're acting as a guide. Sometimes the student gets it right, sometimes wrong; but unless it's some form of mathematics, few things fall neatly into the realm of certainty. Gus, did you throw that pod in the air? Or did you toss it?" Kara wasn't showing off, just letting everyone know teaching wasn't as easy as they may think.

"So, your husband's theory of hidden agendas isn't quite right, is it?" Mirabelle joined the conversation.

"Yes and no," Kara began. "The vast majority of teachers I know try not to impart their personal beliefs on young minds, but some just cannot help themselves. Teachers are human, so of course, they're flawed. Sometimes we just believe certain things so blindly, we insist our students believe them. History and politics definitely fall into that train of thought."

"I can live with that," Gus submitted. "Just watch these news outlets. They've gone away from reporting the news and have turned to spinning headlines like spiders' webs, you don't see the hidden agenda until you're in the spider's grasp. It's like they want to give you your opinion. People are eating it up and conforming to the media's ideals. When you think about it, it seems like a form of brain washing."

"See?" Citalli was standing on the proverbial soap box. "We are what we know and what we perceive. We all know that's a maple tree, we also know that's a beagle, and, uh, we know lunch is getting cold," smirking at the impatience of the crowd to eat, "but, some things we need to decipher for ourselves. You won't know how much that wasp sting hurts until he says hello."

Citalli pointed at Mirabelle's shoulder, she shrieked and swatted it away. Laughter swept the hungry group as they sat down to eat. They decided amongst them that Canneo was free to join them when he felt the ability to break away from his new best friend.

"It's so dry here! I find myself yearning to see more tress, but something in me finds it very peaceful." Gus couldn't help but to admit he enjoyed the times he spent with the Patee family. "I just can't quite put my finger on what it is that I like about this place. Maybe it's just being away from the constant speed and hustle of the city."

"Used to wonder the same thing when I came out here. We must be kindred souls," Citalli said, "because I came to the same conclusion. Of course, I had this one hanging onto to me: 'Oh Citalli'!" Teasing Kara as if she needed him to stay.

"Dream on," She said, "dream on babe. I do that now because your son is a handful."

"You'll be holding on even tighter now. Son and a dog, that's a big handful. I mean, I know he seems like a built-in babysitter now, but puppies have needs." Mirabelle said, trying to let the couple know what they've gotten themselves into.

"I had a house dog as a kid, my dear mother-in-law. I know what I'm doing, and besides, I talked to the breeder and got some pointers. Little Louie there will be kennel trained. Once we have him trained in a few months, it'll be smooth sailing. Think of it this way: you'll have two grandsons waiting for you when you come by, and we'll have a great set of ears that'll hear you coming!" Citalli could barely hold in his laughing as she raised a brow to being told on by the pooch.

"I mean, look at those two," Kara said. "They're going to be best buddies for many years to come. Two peas in a pod!"

"Mom, can I bring Louie over when I eat?" Canneo had no intention of being too far away from Louie.

"You can, as long as your dad holds him while you eat. We have to keep an eye on him until he's trained, baby."

"Bring him," Citalli said, "I need loving from Louie too."

Frantically through the gate, he ran to his father. One word, "Here," Louie was placed in Citalli's hands. Time to dig in, Canneo had already seen the birthday cake waiting for dessert.

Cheeseburgers, plain and dry, with mom's homemade French fries were on the menu first.

Citalli was admiring the pup, gently playing with him while needle sharp teeth nipped at his fingers. He couldn't help but to giggle senselessly like a child, still the silly Citalli. Motioning with his chin for Gus to reach over and pet the new addition, Gus did so. In all the joy of company and conversation, Gus must have momentarily let his guard down as he touched Louie. Citalli noticed his friend suddenly brace himself with an almost fearful look on his face. The happiness-laden smile was momentarily wiped away, then quickly replaced with an obviously troubled smile containing a little something else in it.

Once the party activities were over, and Louie slept snugly in his kennel with Canneo dreaming on the couch next to him, Citalli and Gus decided to relax on the back porch for a bit. Citalli broke out some recently distilled corn liquor, then proceeded to pour a shot glass for himself and his friend.

"Here. You look like you need this," Citalli said with concern in his eyes. "First, we drink, then you decide if you're going to tell me what you saw."

"That obvious, huh? I try to turn it off, really, I do. Usually it controls me more than I control it. You know what, you're right, let's just drink and enjoy some peace and quiet. Give me that." Downing the shot and chasing it with some of Kara's sweet tea. "Thanks, I'm afraid I'm going to need a few more."

"I was hoping you'd say that. Haven't been drunk in a while." Citalli didn't appear to be joking or messing around as he rewarded himself with a drink. "This is an extra stout batch here, so take it easy."

Shot two, shot three, and a fourth shot for good measure! Then, feeling firewater burning in their bellies, the two men went for a stroll back down to the pond. Gus gathered his thoughts through newly acquired focus; or was it from the moonshine?

"An adult Louie was standing right here by the pond while a figure walked into your cornfield there," Gus said pointing to the area. "I couldn't make it out, the figure was blurred. Usually it seems like I get a clear picture, or at least the focal points of the visions are usually clear. It was maybe dusk or dawn; not quite dark. We'll split the difference and say it's either dusk or dawn! The figure was a human shaped shadow, walking upright and moving quietly. It's almost as if it were floating."

Rubbing his chin with his thumb and forefinger Citalli thought to himself for a second. "Could have been anything. The last time you couldn't explain something, at least that I know of, was that ball of light. Remember, no matter how strong the vision, mortal men can never see the true forms divinity. Well, check that; we see what they want us to see. So, do you think it's a good thing you've seen? Can you tell between good and bad?"

"Sometimes." Gus replied, "Not always, but sometimes. All I really saw was the dog barking at the figure, and the figure making its way into the field."

"Cozobi, god of maize, may have been tending my crop. It could be a blessing, it could be something else. As I believe I told you, Canneo is special to the gods. It just seems as though they would watch over him."

"Hard to admit, but you know more about these things than I do. Anyway, I hope you're right. Like I said, the dog was grown.

Those were the only two in the vision. Sometimes, like the time I enlisted you, I'll have additional dreams. If so, I'll let you know."

"Don't be so worried. Just realize, the sooner you can accept we have less control than we think we do, the better you'll be. I mean, even if you believe none of the godly stories I've told you of, even if you put zero stock into religion; you have to know, there's very little we truly control in our lifetimes."

"Of course we have control! Look, people are the caretakers of this planet. We control everything from crops, to animals, to our own atmosphere. You do believe in global warming, don't you?" Gus said, pausing to gesture at all of their surroundings. "If you do, you have to recognize that we created global warming through human inventions. You also have to believe that we can control it."

"That's not control, Gus. We've all played at least some small part in the destruction of our planet, yes. We can and should choose to be responsible, or I guess we could just choose to ignore it. We absolutely know global warming is real, and we absolutely know we caused it. Knowing we caused it gives us some ideas of how to slow or repair it, but we have never controlled it. If we decide, as inhabitants on this rock, that we want to lessen our footprint on it, that will certainly help. As for repairing the planet? Even if we developed a plan, there's no way to action it; the populous simply won't play along. I agree that we have to make a change. Doesn't mean nature has to accept that change. And if you believe, as I do, in the gods; it doesn't mean they should grant us the opportunity to try somewhere else on some distant planet."

"Damn, Citalli! You should drink more." Gus said in a chuckle, clearly impressed by Citalli's rants. "You sound like a voice that needs to be heard tonight. Been sneaking in some late-night reading?

I know that's what I do, I stay awake nights reading and wondering why we choose not to take better care of our planetary home. If there's one instinct we must have held onto, it's self-preservation. Self-preservation to the extent that we care about the future survival of our species. I guess that also goes back to the lack of control. We simply can't control everybody. Those with the need to destroy will find a way; greed seems to be favored over empathy. It all comes down to common sense, I guess. Anyway, don't get me started."

"Sounds like you need another drink, my man!" Citalli said, raising a flask he brought with him.

"Didn't see you grab that when we walked off," Gus said.

"I had a feeling we'd need it. The look in your eyes when we walked this way, I mean, it just kinda tipped me off that things were about to get real."

Gus took an aggressive pull from the flask and passed it back. He then proceeded to walk towards the cornfield. Silence being consent, Citalli followed him. Surely, they weren't looking to see if anyone was there. They walked into the cornfield where Gus stared at the growing stalks.

"Control," he said, "you plant, fertilize, water, and watch. You still need the cooperation of the sun, rain helps reduce watering efforts, though too much can be a detriment. Control."

"If we could just convince the rest of the world, aye? Approach each person, slap them hard enough their ears start ringing, then bend them to our will. Simple right?"

"Well, Citalli, I don't think that type of control will exactly help us. I know sometimes even I consider it the preferred method, but it just doesn't work. Our ancestors, on this continent and beyond, ruled through fear for generations. Seemed like a great idea, but it didn't work."

"Yeah, I suppose I agree with you there, Gus. Somehow, we have to find something between that form of leadership and what we have now. We're not just destroying our planet, we're destroying everything in and on it. Our people have no sense of the world beyond the tip of their nose because they've decided that they're the only thing that matters." Taking another drink and passing the flask, "Let's go back to the house. I need to make sure Canneo gets off the couch goes to bed. I guess I should also make sure that puppy doesn't need to go potty, huh?"

CHAPTER 14

AFTER MAKING SURE HIS MOTHER-IN-LAW MADE IT HOME, CITALLI tucked in Canneo, and of course, Louie. He then watched Gus stumble into the guest room and was finally ready to join Kara in the bedroom. He opened the door slowly in case Kara was asleep, she was not.

"Gustavo saw something else, didn't he? Don't lie either!" Gus's visions were no longer items to be taken lightly as she remembered not only the foresight that led to their meeting, but the way he was able to communicate with the jaguar relic.

"Now, what makes you think I'd lie to you," Citalli said playfully while moving in for a hug and a kiss. "He, uh, he did. He says he saw an adult Louie barking at a figure walking into the cornfield. The figure was blurred, so he doesn't know what it was. He did say it walked upright. Well, actually, he said it kinda glided. It was a brief image and he really doesn't know how to interpret it."

"I don't like the way that sounds, babe. You told me your mother claimed Canneo would be some kind of conduit for Cocijo. You don't think this has anything to do with it, do you?"

"Yeah, that thought occurred to me too. It could be Cozobi, you know, god of maize, checking or blessing our cornfield."

"You don't really believe that do you? An ancient god, I don't care which one, checking the growth of a cornfield?" Kara was beginning to sound a little condescending.

Citalli gave her a look, not sure how the look was being accepted due to his current inebriation. "No, I suppose not. I haven't prayed to my mother since Canneo was born. I was totally spooked when she spoke so clearly about Cocijo, and about Canneo's part in his awakening. My mom, she's always insisted that the gods never wanted sacrifices; insists those were misinterpretations by men, not orders from gods. I don't think she's lying to me, but when I saw Canneo's little face I, I knew I'd do anything to protect him. You have to understand that, don't you?"

"I do, Citalli, you know I do. I see it in your eyes every day. Maybe the only way to know how to protect him is to know just what kind of importance he has. If he's half as important to the gods as he is to us, I'd say he's pretty important. Plus, don't you think your mother would want to protect her grandson?"

"You're right," sinking his head begging for affection. "You're always right girly-girl!" He snickered and snuck in a little kiss. "Remember, no nonsense during prayer, and try to stay positive. I know she'll be disappointed in me, it's been too long."

Kara nodded in agreement, looked into those brown eyes, and gave the man another kiss. He sent a smile her way, breathing it in, savoring the warmth it was delivered with. He then turned his attention to the task at hand, took a deep breath and laid back. Prayers had no ideal position, they required only an attempted communication and a welcoming response. Citalli closed his eyes, placed his palms onto his chest and mentally reached out; no words spoken, just thoughts cascading into the vastness of the beyond.

He loved the tranquil feel of his soul blissfully filling with eternity. He eased slowly into what felt like dream and awakened in the same cloud-like translucent room of prayer. His image projected into a prayer vessel along with the image of his mother's spirit. There was no sound, yet somehow there seemed to be no feeling of silence either.

"Mijo! Ten years! You make me wait ten years?!" Apparently, members of the spirit world were still able to get a little upset.

"I'm sorry mother. I'm so sorry. Little Canneo is everything to me, and I've been afraid that when Cocijo awakens he'll be taken from me."

"Now, that's not how it works, mijo. Cocijo will awaken with or without Canneo. Canneo will absorb much of the lightning god's fury, this is meant to allow Cocijo time to calm himself. Canneo is a conduit, a blessing given to you from the gods, and he is the future of our people. He will not be harmed, mijo, he will be protected."

"How mom? How can he possibly absorb the lightning god's fury and not be harmed? I feel his blessings every day, I know he's a blessing, but, absorbing lightning from Cocijo himself, I just can't see surviving that."

"Faith, mijo. He survives it with faith, his and yours. Understanding is not always important when it comes to the wills and ways of gods. I have watched as you and your wife raise little Canneo, and I know he has love. You have taught him the importance of faith and have told him of the gods. As a young boy, he believes what you tell him and one day he will see with his own eyes; you will see, with your own eyes."

She paused for a moment, observing the overwhelming signs of concern on his face. "I caught your discussion on control, mijo."

"Ah," he said with a renewed humor in his eyes, "so, you do watch over me? OK then, let's hear it!"

"You despair too much, mijo. You do not have to accept a total lack of control. You control what you think, what you say, what you do. In these ways you influence the world around you. Yes, your crops need rain and sunshine; but, had you not planted the seeds, then there would be no plants at all. Well, at least, there would be no field of maize. So, you see? The control you seek outside of your deeds becomes influence and action. Try not to get too upset about a lack of control."

"Any advice on how the world goes about controlling climate change, then? I mean, it's real, isn't it? There must be an answer here, in the heavens." Now, Citalli thought to himself, time to fish around for a fresh perspective. A perspective that came from a world beyond his own.

"Control!" She hit him with his own words and a wink. "Of course, there has to be control! This is not mine to control; it's not yours to control. Mankind has a penchant for destruction. Mankind's leaders have always cared more about power and wealth than they have about anything or anyone else; chalk it up to human nature."

"Now we're getting somewhere, ha-ha," Citalli said through the laughter. "First, I can only control me, then we make the whole planet care through influenced control. I like it! Tell me more."

"You know better than that, Citalli. Please, sit."

Through Citalli's childlike rant came a maternal instinct to calm her son. Hesitantly, as if pondering whether or not he needed to calm down, Citalli sat. He crouched slightly forward, placed his elbows on his knees and clasped his palms together. Taking a couple of deep breaths to calm himself, he moved his hands to rub his face and eyes before looking up again.

"Tell me about Canneo, mijo. Tell me about my grandson," she said.

Now there's something that sky-rocketed a smile on his face. Picturing the boy, he started, "I know you've watched over us, and I thank you for that."

"I am but spirit now, mijo. Tell me, through a father's eyes. Tell me through your eyes."

"His eyes are the deepest, darkest brown. Kara describes them as mahogany because of the fiery reddish tint. You can only see it if the light allows you to. We cut his hair very short. He likes it that way; it keeps him cool. Sometimes you can tell by his facial expression what's getting ready to happen, and it's almost always something silly. He's smart, much smarter than me. Nature and animals are definitely his favorite subjects. Birds, trees, coyotes and bobcats running by; they all capture his imagination. We're just now starting to work on poetry with him, it's not exactly his favorite subject. As you can guess, most of his poems have been about the natural wonders around him."

"Of course! The world around him calls to him as it does any child. Sadly, we can never recapture the innocence we saw the world through as children. Life changes us, it's meant to. Please try to remember this, Citalli, enjoy his youth."

"When will Cocijo awaken, mother? You said Canneo would see it, you said I would see it. So, when?"

"Try not to dwell on that, mijo. They will awaken Cocijo in due time, it will still be a matter of years. The gods work at the pace the gods work, these things take a while. I do not know the intentions of the gods, and I am in no position to question them. I must praise them and honor them. They have chosen to bless my grandson, and this makes me happy."

"So, you're not nervous about it at all? Cocijo's power is going to be passing through Canneo's body, and you're not worried?"

"Maybe because I am part of the spirit world now, maybe that gives me more perspective, because I can see past earthly fears. Neither you nor I can know the will of the gods, and we certainly cannot change it. Some things you must just accept. Canneo is a good boy because you have taught him to be, and he will continue to be who you teach him to be. Someday, when he becomes a man, he will find his own way. Just like you did."

"And the ancient jaguar stone you gave me? Does that have any-thing to do with this?" Citalli still has more questions than answers.

"Your mystical friend was able to communicate with the stone, I know. When I gave you that stone, it was something that had been passed down many generations. Honestly, I knew little about it in life; only that it was special. It holds no magic, mijo. Well, at least not anymore."

"So, it was powerful or magical, mother? It really caused a man to turn into a jaguar? Naguals were real? I guess my biggest question is: do naguals still exist?"

"There were two stones mijo, one of hessonite and one of onyx. They were crafted in Lyobaa and blessed by a priest named Danaà. Danaà was uija-tào, the great seer. Much like your friend Gustavo, Danaà had visions. These visions were of the stars and of the gods. Danaà made many prophecies, including that of a nagual; the very nagual your friend told you about. The ceremony Gus witnessed was the rite of passage for the boy to transfer into his spirit animal.

When the boy returned to human form, his passage into manhood was complete. And as to if they still exist, yes. But a nagual cannot take the form of its spirit animal until it receives a blessing from the gods. This blessing has not been given in many years; centuries."

"You taught me," Citalli started, "That all living creatures had a spirit. So, does the man take the spirit of a jaguar, or does the jaguar take the spirit of a man?"

"A man is a man; a beast is a beast. Some nagual are allowed to share the visions and senses of their spirit beast, like a kindred spirit. Some men are born with the spirit of the beast inside them, these men may change themselves into the beast; but they must receive a blessing from the gods. Naguals are not just linked to the jaguar, they come in many forms. Wolves, foxes, coyotes, and birds of all kinds just to name a few. As you said, all living things have spirits."

Feeling lucky, Citalli poised himself for the question that perplexed him the most. A question he's wanted to ask for an entire decade, one that might just make sense of this whole ten-year journey. "Is Gustavo the new uija-tào? He has visions but doesn't know his lineage, besides the fact that he's of Mexican descent."

"I find myself wondering this as well. I have prayed to the gods and asked this question. It would make sense to have an uija-tào to converse with the gods once Cocijo has awakened. The gods tell me what I tell you, be patient and in time all will be revealed."

"Be patient and accept that which I control. Try to influence that which I don't control. That's the whole message? Mother, that's not a whole lot to go off of."

"There are no other answers, mijo. The message is that Cocijo and the rest of the gods will pass judgment when Cocijo has been awakened, and not a moment before. Canneo is a blessing from the gods and will be a blessing for our people. The gods will judge, Citalli; that's all that is known."

"How do I go forward then? Knowing that judgment is coming, and not just someday … but soon."

"Mijo, you think of judgment in terms of Armageddon. Judgment does not mean the end of life, it just means judgment. This is for Cocijo and the others to decide. Has mankind gone astray? Yes. Does that mean all of mankind should pay the ultimate price? I don't know that. Cocijo has slumbered and dreamed for many years, but he still sees. Judgment could be good, bad or anywhere in between. Mijo, it could be nothing at all."

"Neither of us believe it will be nothing at all, be honest!" Citalli snapped back.

"Agreed, but the point is we don't know. What we do know is that Cocijo will return, and that you will teach Canneo to be a man. You will teach Canneo, descendant of Cocijo, to be the servant of Cocijo."

"I will teach him to be a man because I love him, because I am his father, and because we are both descended from Cocijo. I'll honor Cocijo by developing my son to be respectful, wise and educated. I'll show Cocijo that there are things in this world that are still worth his blessings. Just because mankind has grown in an unpleasant manner, does not mean we're completely lost. There are good people out there, mother!"

"I know, Citalli. I am looking at a good man right now. My son, my star, my blessing. My earthly life has passed without knowing the blessings of Cocijo, embrace his return. Peoples from other parts of the world do not believe as we do, don't concern yourself with their views of judgment or of divinity. This will be a blessing, mijo; remember that."

"You could have led with that," Citalli said with his signature child-like charm. "We talked about things I always thought would be horrible. Should I be convinced that they won't be?"

"You should be convinced that control, at least of the gods' will, is not yours. There is a difference in being descended from Cocijo and being Cocijo. Now, do not wait so long to bless me with your prayers."

She brushed her hand lovingly form one shoulder blade to the next, then back to the center, ending with a firm squeeze to the base of the neck. The squeeze seemed to blur his vision and begin to remove his projection from the prayer vessel. As illumination turned to blur and blur to dark, Citalli was swept into dream. He would wake later, in Kara's loving arms.

CHAPTER 15

April 22, 2019
Taugui, Oklahoma

GATHERED AROUND THE DINNER TABLE HAVING JUST ENJOYED their meal, the Patee family was preparing itself for the annual planting season. Citalli had been out most of the day plowing the field in preparation for planting before midday tomorrow. After all, there were other preparations to be made. The seed to be sown must be soaked overnight and that Lyrid meteor shower wasn't going to watch itself!

"When do the meteors start again, Dad?" Canneo was nearly sixteen and developing a deeper tone of voice. He still possessed that boyish smile and a heart of solid gold.

"Well, you'll probably be able to see a stray meteor or two later on this evening, but the payoff comes a few hours before dawn; that's the best time. We'll take a peak later, hit the sack early, then get up about three or so to enjoy the show." Getting a fifteen-year-old boy up at that time of morning wouldn't be easy, but Citalli felt up to the task. The two had watched the annual event every year its view was not obstructed by the clouds.

"Well, before you watch that meteor shower with your father, you owe me some homework Canneo Patee!" Ever the teacher, his mother wasn't about to let him slide. She knew many young modern men shied away from poetry but reminded Canneo that many of the most celebrated poets were indeed men. Still, the boy felt a little uncomfortable expressing himself in such a manner.

"I have a surprise for you then, mom. I've written a masterpiece! That's right, Canneo Patee, poet and didn't know it." The room reverberated with laughter between the three of them. Homeschooling just had a way of involving the entire family; teaching, in and of itself, was a very effective means of learning through the eyes of the pupil.

The boy ran into his room, charged back out and stated, "I want to read this out loud. I'm serious, I really think it's good!"

His parents looked at each other, sharing a prideful smile, and instructed Canneo to continue. Citalli egged him on with some applause.

With a serious look on his face Canneo took looked down at the paper, gave a cough to clear the airway, then began:

"Of the earth, of clouds, or of the sky,
Where legends live and foes, they die;

Our deeds our greatness we carved in stone,
A king from gods sits 'pon the throne;

Peaks of hills carved for the gods,
Our lands too dry, we beat the odds;

Obsidian blades cut flesh from bone,
Our might our strength our fury be known;

We lived for love and died for glory,
In legend now resides our story;

When through the night our fires burn,
Our gods will see and soon return. "

Then, taking a deep breath to remove himself from the scenery introduced in his poem, Canneo looked up as if demanding approval.

"Wow! I'm impressed Canneo! Here I thought you didn't like poetry. Citalli?" Clearly impressed not only by her son's work, but by the pride he showed in it, she passed the mantle of recognition to her husband.

Citalli was staring down at the table and clearly taken aback at the boy's recognition of his bloodlines. He could see the greatness of Monte Albàn and its inhabitants through words elaborately displayed by his son. "It's like you can see them, Canneo. I could see them through your eyes." He looked up showing eyes welling up with fought back tears, with pride and something else; concern. "Can you see them, Son? Have you seen the city in your dreams?"

"Everybody dreams, dad! Of course, I've seen the city, you showed me pictures. The only differences between the pictures and my dreams are that people are in the city."

"Really? Touristy people? Elders? Sit down, tell me about it," Citalli insisted in an encouraging manner. "So, how come you never mentioned this before?"

The young man sat down directly next to his father, feeling the deep connection he'd always shared with him. Citalli grabbed his hand as if to motion him to begin, then winked.

"The city was still in ruins like it is today, but people were rebuilding it, I think. It's like people were living there. Silly, huh? I mean, I know it's a historical site, they wouldn't just let people move back in, would they?"

Citalli's heart was stuck in his throat blocking air and speech. Was this a dream or a vision? Should he tell the boy about the awakening? That would be a little difficult not knowing exactly when it would occur, not to mention it could burden his son with undue anxiety over the event. But then again, maybe the anxiety was a necessary obstacle. Cocijo was coming, and Canneo would be the one to feel his power and presence.

"Ahem," composing himself, Citalli leaned and looked into Canneo's eyes. "Son, do you believe the stories of the gods I share with you?"

Kara shot her husband a sideways glance. They agreed Canneo would know when the time was right, but was it? Was this the time?

Keeping his hand firmly on Canneo's, he reached his other to Kara's. Kara squeezed as if in prayer for mercy. "Do you, son?" Citalli said softly demanding a response.

"Yes, dad, I do. I know in my mind they're real. It's like some-one's talking to me sometimes when I sleep. I can hear the voices, but I can't make out what they say. They don't scare me, they talk like, I don't know; it just seems like they care. I know how that sounds, but they're not angry voices."

Assuredly smiling now, a tear made its way down Citalli's cheek. "We're descended from Cocijo, son. We do not believe like many other religions believe; that they we're created by their gods. We are truly descended from our gods, from Cocijo. He's been sleeping for centuries, you see; and I believe what you hear are the incantations of other gods awakening him."

Seeing his father weeping, Canneo knew they were far removed from joking. "But dad, how can you know that? You said it yourself, we don't know the will of the gods."

"In prayer, son. It was revealed to me on the day of your birth and confirmed on your tenth birthday. I'm told that when the lightning god appears, you'll be, well, let's just say you're important. I'm not sure how it all works, but you're an important part of the awakening."

A smile from the boy. It was as if he knew something, "I've seen us, but we're not here. I don't know where we are. A ditch, maybe a crater, something like that. Its dark, clouds roll in from nowhere like in a movie. Lightning fills the clouds, and I don't mean just a little. I can feel you, mom and Gus."

Kara placed her forehead atop Citalli's clenched fist in an attempt to conceal her tears. Citalli kissed the hair on the crown of her head to soothe her emotions. "What do you mean feel us? And Gus, too?"

"Yeah … I mean, I don't know. Somehow, I can feel that you're there, but I can't see you. I guess I always thought it was a dream. Does this mean I have visions like Gus?"

"I honestly don't know what it means, son. All we know is that Cocijo will awaken, and you're the … well, you're important. If you don't see pain, death or destruction … that's a good thing! What I say is that you're a fifteen, almost sixteen-year-old descendant of Cocijo. And I also say its time you had a drink with the old man on the porch!"

Kara didn't drink and never really approved of Citalli's drinking. Tonight, she needed a drink; maybe five or six, maybe she should lose count. Citalli grabbed an unopened bottle of the good stuff while Kara and Canneo began placing the corn seeds into a trough of water alongside the back porch. Best to get this done before washing down distilled spirits designed to numb the senses. There would be no need for a three o'clock wake up, they both knew Citalli's drinking went straight through the night.

"On second thought, forget the porch! Let's sit out at the picnic table and let Louie sniff around, huh?" Citalli proposed to the group. "We may need his senses when ours fade." Smiling before the two of them had their first drink.

Now full-grown, thirteen-inches at the shoulder, Louie was six-year-old beagle in his prime. Ever Canneo's best friend, the two had become inseparable. He trotted out the door and did what hound dogs do; sniffed, barked and rubbed his back on the grass. The three of them could watch him for hours as he worked, came over for some attention, and then went back to work again.

As the Gibbous moon became more prominent in the night sky, the celestial entertainment began. Lack of a moon would make for a better display as darker skies revealed more meteors, but something about the moon has always enticed the imagination of mortal men.

The meteors streaked through the sky about a good ten minutes apart, giving enough time for a shot of Dad's liquor, some sweet tea to chase it down, and a refocusing on the heavens. Citalli's eyes grew bigger as he awaited the occasional meteor that carried with it an ionized gas trail.

"And what's that called again, son?" He'd ask the boy, applauding the correct answer that always found its way into their stargazing.

"It's called a persistent train! That one I always remember because I imagine a train following the meteor, ha-ha!" Good times! This was father son time at its best because this time, mom joined them for stargazing.

Watching the heavenly display until the sun's pitch was visible on the horizon, Canneo paused to impart some more of his knowledge of the stars on his mother. "See mom, the waning gibbous moon is still visible after the sun rises." The boy, like his mother, drank slowly through the night. Citalli, of course, was a professional; meaning they had to make him stop about an hour ago.

"I don't think we'll be awake until later this afternoon. Think we should get busy planting?" Citalli was preparing for the headache to come.

"Sure, babe. We'll be good and tired by the time we're done. I'm so thankful you never wanted a bigger plot planted."

Draining the seeds and placing them into cotton shoulder sacks, the three headed towards the recently plowed field. The warmth of the morning sun shone light on the field as if offering an invitation into the field to be sown. Humming and staggering, the three of them began the process of planting. Two seeds were sown about every twelve inches and into straight lines. Placing the seeds, then covering them with rich soil before moving to the next took time and patience. After the first dozen or so mounds had been sown, a rhythmic sort of motion began and allowed for greater speed and precision. Sure, there were easier ways to do this, but the rewards were sweeter when the seeds were lovingly placed.

Louie, apparently done sniffing around, found himself a spot to lay down directly in the sun. Time to watch the humans do a little work. He lay there with his eyes squinted almost closed soaking up the warmth of the sun. His head turned and his ears raised, what was coming from the tall grass?

Standing about ten inches tall and walking slightly lunged forward. Mostly brown with black spots and streaks, the roadrunner makes his living hunting. Savagely competent hunters, roadrunners do not limit themselves to insects and the like, but are also known to east mice, lizards, frogs and snakes. Their demeanor has always made them a revered predator among the people native to this continent.

"A roadrunner," said Citalli. "Let's watch! Canneo, what can you tell me about the roadrunner?"

"They can run up to twenty-six miles per hour, they only have limited flight, and they inhabit the United States and Mexico," Canneo replied.

"Remember, all living things have a spirit, son. It's been whispered among our people that roadrunners hold magical powers over people. Maybe we think that because of the fact that we become so entranced by them, they're such impressive predators. I mean, just look at the guy!"

Canneo always noticed how philosophical his father got when he had a little too much to drink. It was almost like he spoke better when that artificial fire burned within him, and it was hilarious.

The predatory bird stopped, paused and slightly spread its wings as if egging something on. As the unmistakable sound of rattling carried on the wind, it became apparent a fight to the death was imminent. Canneo quickly ran over and picked up Louie just in case the nosy little hound got curious.

Circling the snake, the roadrunner occasionally dipped and lunged, drawing the snake's ire. The snake rattled and hissed in warning as he timed his lunges with the bird's advances. A dart by the bird, a lunge by the snake; a dance to the death for one of them. The roadrunner quickly dove and retreated as the snake snapped at him, a flap of the wing led the bird back in before the snake's retraction. The bird grabbed the snake by the top half of its open mouth. With a powerful grip and twist, the roadrunner bashed the snake's head on the ground repeatedly, and relentlessly, until the snake's body went as limp.

"Well," Citalli said, reaching over to pat Louie on the head, "someone's watching over us! That rattler didn't stand a chance."

Kara was awestricken as well, what a show of skill! After witnessing the conclusion of the hunt, she turned to Canneo. "Why don't you and Louie go in the house and get some sleep. Your father and I can finish up here, right Dad?"

"Good idea! We're almost done anyway. Close your door so Louie doesn't run back out here. Best to make sure there was only one snake."

After Canneo and Louie made their way into the house, true to their word the couple finished planting and made a sweep of the area. Any common snake would not be such a big deal, but rattlers were well known for killing their victims.

"Babe, are you sure Canneo was ready to hear his future?" Kara said. "I thought we would at least talk about it before we told him."

"I know," Citalli started, "I let that poem get to me, I guess. But it sounded like he already knew more about it than we did. Those were visions, not dreams! The fact that he saw visions of anything but destruction, let's just say I think that's a good thing."

"You do realize, you're going to have to call Gus now?" Overstating the obvious to her husband.

"Yeah, I'm thinking that should happen soon, too. Not that I have any idea how this is going to go, but if he's hearing the divine language of the gods, it would kinda make sense that we're getting close."

Kara looked around and pointed to their recently completed work. "Gus saw Louie barking at a figure in the cornfield, I guess that gives us a couple of months at least."

"You're assuming it's happening this year," Citalli said. "All we know is that it is going to happen, and that its going to happen in our lifetime. Gus's vision aside, we're kinda jumping to conclusions."

"I need to know, babe. There's only one person on this earth that I know of with the ability to see this stuff. He's not just our friend, he's Canneo's godfather! That gives him a right to know. I think you should call him while Canneo sleeps."

Taking her in his arms, "You win. You always win. Not just that, you're always right. Come on, let's go call Gussy-Gus."

Not a word was spoken during the short walk back to the house. Making it inside, they peaked inside the boy's room to see the two compadres sleeping.

It took a whopping two rings for Gus to answer, "Hey, stranger! I was wondering when I would hear from you. Sweet sixteen is coming real soon, is this my official invite?"

"It's good to hear your voice," Citalli said. "It's been too long, buddy."

"Something wrong?" Citalli's shortness and lack of enthusiasm raised immediate concerns.

"Ah, just got in from planting the maize, uh, corn. We stayed up drinking all night watching the meteors, then went straight to planting. So, I'm drunk and I'm tired," Citalli said with a controlled and muffled laugh.

"I hope you saved some of that for me!" Gus replied.

"Plenty more where that came from. You know Kara only lets me drink a couple times a year. Anyway, yes, we'd like you to come see us. As a matter of fact, the sooner the better."

A brief silence, the pause did not come unexpectedly. "Something happened, didn't it? Last night I dreamt of the vision I had, you know, the one with Louie and the cornfield. That was the first time I was visited by that dream since, well … since Canneo's tenth birthday."

"Canneo's having dreams too Gus," Citalli said. "I believe they're visions. I'd like to talk to you about it, but not over the phone. You understand."

"Just so happens you're in luck, buddy. My retirement recently approved, and I was kinda waiting to tell you. Anyway, Friday's my last day before I'm granted the freedom of retirement. I could be there Saturday, will that work?"

Looking at Kara, Citalli replied, "Kara said that would be awesome," winking at her. "It'll give her time to get the guestroom ready and clean this mess up!" Gus could hear a muffled and playful smack through the phone. It was nice to know time hadn't changed the couple.

CHAPTER 16

Saturday, April 27, 2019

RETIRED LIFE! GUS THOUGHT HE MUST HAVE WAITED A LIFETIME to finally give up the daily grind associated with his work. Maybe it was just time to concentrate on his memoirs. Nothing that needed to be published, but just something to reflect upon his professional life along with the personal relationships built along the way. Now back in Oklahoma, the most meaningful personal relationship of his many years was in need of his presence. It was nice to feel needed.

Gus decided before he left the big city that it would be nice to rent a vehicle instead of having Citalli pick him up at the airport. He opted for what he considered a sporty little minivan, red in color. He thought the extra space would come in handy should they decide to have some form of family outing.

He drove the minivan past the city and military installation, then into the silence laden backroads of Taugui. A smile grew across his face as he remembered his first visitation of the area, glaring out the window of Citalli's muscle car into the never-ending grasslands of the prairie; the area once referred to as the last frontier. Wasn't that a joke? It seems there will always be a new frontier. We still knew more about outer space than we did about our own oceans; or at least, we thought we did.

He thought back to the conversation in the cornfield during his last visit six years past. Control! The topic of conversation tunneled through his mind for weeks before he could chase it away. The very thought that they had no control over what was coming made that conversation populate his thoughts in a near desperate manner. Control.

Pulling into the driveway at the Patee residence, he noticed a tall skinny young man playing in the yard with a now adult beagle. Canneo and Louie had both grown, and apparently were still just as inseparable as they were the day they became pals.

Parking the van and opening the door, Gus noticed Louie racing towards the van playfully barking. Louie was just a pup during his last visit, not a chance he remembered Gus. As he closed the door of the van, Canneo was fast on Louie's heels and rushing the van. "Gus!" Canneo ran to Gus and gave him a bear hug.

Gus, never one to let his emotions get the best of him, returned the hug with all the love a man could muster. "Wow! You've grown so tall, and still such a handsome young man! And this must be Louie clawing at my leg!" Hind legs on the ground, Louie was standing with his front two paws planted firmly on Gus's left thigh.

Laughing that same silly laugh, the boy said, "Louie likes his loving too. Nobody comes over without getting the once over, then loving on him. C'mon, Mom and Dad are in the house."

The old house hadn't changed much, the years of wear seemed to give it an even more eclectic feel. Louie led the way, apparently knowing where everyone was going. He would look back from time to time, kind of making sure the two stayed on course.

"The front door doesn't work very good anymore, we'll use the back, ok?" Canneo said, giving a gesture towards the back of the house.

"I thought your dad was a real mister fix it kinda guy. What's up with that?" Gus said jokingly.

"Dad says it's a blessing in disguise. Something about people not being able to sneak up on us anymore. But that hasn't been a problem since we got Louie. Isn't that right boy?" The whole family tended to talk to the dog as if talking to a baby, and he always seemed to give facial expressions as if answering. Sometimes, just like any other person, those expressions were loaded.

Approaching the back door, they paused a second or two so Gus could admire the pond. Staring into that pond, Gus thought to himself, made the world seem smaller and less complicated. Within the waters of the pond lie its own personal ecosystem. Survival of the fittest, yes; but gluttony could come back to haunt you in the most horrific way. Feed but conserve. How did they manage it? Was instinct enough? When did mankind lose its instinctual habits?

Deep in thought for what seemed like an eternity, Gus looked up and noticed Citalli rushing out of the back door. "Gussy-Gus! The Gusmeister!" Another manly bear hug to greet him. "How was your trip?" Asked Citalli without giving Gus a chance to answer. "Man, it's been so long! Kara's taking a nap, how about we have a seat under the old maple, huh?"

"Sounds good," said Gus, "took me three different flights to get here, that crop dusting pad you call an airport only lets in the smallest of aircraft. All the same, I really am going to miss the perks of government transport! Anyway, open space and fresh air is what I need."

Gus, Citalli and Canneo all three stopped to pick up a maple seed pod as if it were a mutual call to action. Smiling at one another to signal their likeness of thought, they sat down at the old picnic table. They each held their helicopter pod between thumb and forefinger examining it, Canneo reached his out for Louie to have a sniff. Louie took a brief inspection of the pod and turned his attention to Gus. Putting his ears back in an exuberant manner, he placed his front paws atop Gus's lap and gave him a look.

"Told you," Canneo said, "he's going to get that loving!"

And that he did! Gus placed his hand on the scruff of Louie's neck and began to rub and pet him. Amazingly, he thought, he found himself speaking to the dog in an affectionate tone of baby mutterings. Awe heck, just go with it!

"So, retired man now, huh?" Citalli set in. "Any immediate plans? I mean, besides the obvious."

"I've thought about it a little," Gus started, "Besides writing some form of personal memoir, not really. I wouldn't mind donating some of my savings for a country plot like this. Some peace and quiet after years deploying to one continent and then the next, that would be nice." Looking down at his new furry friend, "Maybe Mister Louie would come keep me company, huh buddy?" Tongue hanging out and a look of affection, Louie seemed all in.

"We could find you a noble companion, or maybe even give you visitation rights with Louie; but understand, that's a family member. And the only reason you would qualify for visitation is that you're a family member too." Citalli said, confirming Gus's place within the grand scheme of things.

"Citalli, my friend," Gus said, "I've got a six pack on ice in the van. What say you and I head down to the pond for a while to discuss recent goings on."

"Well, since you asked so nicely," Citalli grinned and motioned, "Let's move out! Son, you and Louie go in catch up on some TV time. Please keep the noise down; remember, your mom's sleeping."

The two groups went their separate ways. Canneo knew he would be the topic of discussion, but also knew they had his best interests in mind. Louie, on the other hand, could sleep half the day without skipping a beat.

Making it down to the shores of the pond, it was beer time! But what was this? Gus broke out a six pack of sodas instead of the ceremonial brew. Well at least he brought some rootbeer in real glass bottles. The twist, pop, and the fizz of the bottles led to a manly clanking of bottles in a toasting motion. "To your family," Gus said.

"Our family," Citalli replied. "And to your retirement. You deserve it, you've served your country and should be proud of that."

Drinking ice cold rootbeer and staring into the placid water of the pond seemed to intensify the yearning for an explanation of recent and coming events. What they knew, or at least what they thought they knew, was that Cocijo would be awakening soon. Also, it was becoming more and more apparent that Canneo may be just a little bit more than a conduit. He could hear what Citalli interpreted to be the divine language of the gods.

"Control," Gus blurted out of nowhere.

"Come again?" Citalli said. "What do you mean, control?"

"The last time I was here, you articulated every single angle of the word control. Speaking of our need for it, our illusion of it and our undoing by the lack of it. That drove me nuts for weeks," he said exercising a whimsical laugh. "You did some serious damage to my psyche with rantings about control."

Joining in on the laughter that seemed create a ripple in the still waters of the pond Citalli added, "Dude, I was drunk. I rambled on so long I gave myself a headache. Then launched myself into a pretentious prayer meeting with my mother about the perception of control. You remember, I told you about it."

"Yeah-yeah, Citalli, I remember. And your prayers lately?"

"We still meet in prayer. She's never led me too far off of the right path. Look, I know she tells me every bit of truth she knows; but even she admits she doesn't know the will of the gods. She doesn't know if the collective attitude of the gods will change when Cocijo returns."

Pondering his friend's answer, he sat down near the water's edge. "So, what did she tell you about why he came to be in this sleep-like state? Angry, vengeful, disappointed? Just plain tired, maybe?"

"The gods, not just Cocijo, were angered by, I don't know, call it a lack of respect, maybe even a lack of unity. Elites claimed to be the true and only descendants of the gods," Citalli said looking like he was getting slightly upset. "They used the power to create fear and obedience. Anyway, the gods believed that the most worthy of mankind on this continent would survive to create a new society, a new reality."

"And they didn't get it I'm guessing?" Gus asked, knowing the answer.

"Exactamente, Gustavo! Sacrifice, bloodletting and mutilating of body parts; these were not the wishes or demands made by the gods. These we inventions of men hell bent on destruction and intoxicated by nothing more than bloodlust. The gods just let it go because, the way I understand it, they were hedging their bets on a clear-cut winner. Which tribe won was unimportant; the unification of the Mesoamerican populous was the goal. Seeing no way out of the never-ending cycle, Cocijo enlisted Pecala, god of dreams, to place him in an extended repose."

"And during this repose, his people were conquered and enslaved. And the rest of the gods? They didn't see fit to intervene?" Gus was asking the same questions Citalli had asked many years ago.

"I know it seems harsh, Gus. Gods don't interfere as much as you think. The will of the gods follows the path of mankind. A decision was made to have no more interference until Cocijo awakened. Besides, I think they've only intervened twice: once with us, and once with a priest protecting the temple to the underworld in what we know today as Mitla."

"Twice in at least five centuries, huh? Not to mention a third time upcoming," Gus said.

Citalli pulled a small flask from his pocket, "Some of the good stuff?"

Still trying to get a grip and searching for words, Gus welcomed the sight of something a little stronger than rootbeer. Grabbing the flask form Citalli's hand, he nodded deliberately before being interrupted.

"Drinking's not going to help you, Gus!" A feminine voice said from behind him.

"Kara!" Gus jumped to his feet and gave her a friendly hug. "Now, you should know better than to sneak up behind two men that are up to no good."

"I should, but I want a coherent vision," she said. "The only way I'm going to get that is to barter for a stoppage of your, um, activities."

"So, you're sure that's what you want? I mean, look, I'm almost always right when it comes to human interfacing, but my clairvoyance has a way of hitting some serious static when dealing with divinity. Not to mention, are you sure you want to put little Canneo through this?"

She turned and looked sadly at Citalli, as if wanting him to speak; he had nothing. Grabbing Gus's hand, "As you can see, he's not so little anymore. As Citalli told you, he's getting visions and hearing incantations we believe to be from the gods. If what you've seen is coming this year, basically, we have the growing season; give or take."

Looking off into the distance by the house, Gus noticed Canneo and Louie playfully running in the backyard. Gus gave a wave to gain their attention, then motioned them over. "The vision included Louie somewhere in this area looking towards the cornfield. Any objections to trying to get a reading here?"

The two looked at one another and shook their heads in declination. Free of the burden of objection, Gus approached Canneo.

"You know why I'm here, godson?" He said almost beneath his breath.

The boy smiled, "Of course! You have visions, like I do."

"Well, kinda," Gus started. "My visions require the sensation of touch. I've worked for many years to suppress it. I now know that's impossible, but I have gained better control of it over these past few years. I'm not sure if that'll give me a better vision, or any vision at all, but we should try if you're ready."

Still the same old Canneo; never much for words he smiled, nodded and held out his hand. Gus detailed some of the things he may feel while a reading was extracted and assured him of his safety during it, all of which the boy took in stride. Amazing how the young were so brave and care free.

Taking a deep breath and slowly closing his eyes, Gus reminded the group it would require only their silence. He grabbed Canneo's hand and was unsuspectedly jolted and thrust into vision; no pause and certainly no transition.

The vision was consumed by the darkness of night and illuminated only by shooting stars catapulting through the sky. As before, Louie stood on all four by the pond barking at a dark figure. Canneo entered the vision now, emerging from behind Louie and approached as if drawn by the figure. Gus squinted and peered, but the figure still revealed only a shadowy form. A shadowy form that was seemingly absorbed by the cornfield.

The likeness of Canneo moved to the edge of the cornfield while Louie followed closely behind, barking incessantly. One in front of the other, the two approached the cornfield, Canneo seemed entranced by it. Walking into the field, Canneo's figure disappeared and the dog followed, silently now.

Ability to move freely about was often granted in Gus's visions, it was no different in this one. He scurried quickly over to the patch of corn, which at closer inspection appeared ready for harvest. Canneo slowly and almost obediently lay himself on the ground. Louie was sitting silently beside him, staring at him.

There were two dark figures now. The first was the same as seen from afar, appearing to be a shadow in the shape of a man.

No manly features adorned his frame, no eyes, ears or mouth, just shadow.

The second figure, while initially blurry and hazy, slowly became more colorful and vibrant. Appearing in the shape of a man, he was equal in height to Gus and staring straight eye to eye as if wanting to be seen. He carried the complexion of the indigenous peoples of the Americas. He wore a gold mesh pelt and was adorned with lavish paint covering all but his head. This resulted in making him glow a brilliant golden color. His headdress was made of what could only be described as pennaceous feathers fashioned from pure jade; the vanes and barbules were consistent with that of a real feather but glittered of jade. Within the headdress there appeared to be some form of electrical current, perhaps lightning. Along the band of the headdress were gleaming golden husks of corn.

Gus was absolutely dumbfounded. Frozen in his stance, he was in the presence of the supernatural. He glanced away form the being and observed Canneo lying on the ground with eyes open, obviously alive but placed under some form of reverie. As he glanced back to the phenomena before him, the shadow advanced engulfing him as a fog would; then darkness.

CHAPTER 17

CREEPING BACK TO CONSCIOUSNESS GUS OPENED HIS EYES. HE was lying in bed with Citalli sitting beside him. "How did I get here?"

Perking up with childlike enthusiasm Citalli said, "We carried you! Man, you were out cold. We actually considered calling an ambulance, but it seemed like you were just asleep. One moment you were holding Canneo's hand, then you hit the dirt like a sack of potatoes. Here, drink this and try to relax," Citalli handed him a bottle of water, "doctor's orders. Doctor being me."

Gus propped himself up to a seated position, shrugging off offers of help in doing so. He pulled slowly and repetitively from the bottle, tapping into his memory stores at the chain of events witnessed in his vision. "Well, bring everyone in here. I think all of you should hear it."

No sooner had he got the words out, then the other two appeared in the doorway, and Louie jumped on the bed. Concerned eyes drew upon him as faint smiles seemingly greeted him back to the land of the living. Kara was bringing a bowl of some form of subsistence, he waved it off and she set it at his bedside. "Everybody sit down, I'm fine," said Gus.

185

Drawing upon freshly-minted memories, Gus began to tell them of the vision, and of the two fascinating figures he witnessed in the vision. He kept repeating the fact that he had never been noticed by any living creature in his visions. "Never, Citalli. Never," he quipped. "I can still see the intense gaze of immortality in his eyes. Almost as if he could see forever and beyond, demanding my fear; he wasn't just demanding my fear, he got it."

Looking to the ground, partially in thought and partially in fear, Citalli said, "So Canneo was lying there, Louie was calm, and you got the sense the two figures wanted you to see that, huh? The gods revealed themselves to you for a reason, Gus. I know you've shown a lot of reservation about my beliefs over the years, but you have to believe now, don't you?"

"I believe what I saw. I believe them to be supernatural beings, gods if you like. But the real question is this: why render him unconscious in the middle of your field if Canneo's visions include some form of crater?"

"I don't know," said Citalli, "but I have a pretty good idea who it was you saw. Cozobi, god of maize, matches the description of the figure staring at you. Can't really say who described him first, mortals aren't supposed to be able to see the gods; maybe some ancient event kinda mirrored this one, who knows?"

"And the other one?" Said Gus. "The other one remained in shadow, like a dark cloud."

"That's the easy one Gus," Citalli laughed. "He put you to sleep when he surrounded you. Pecala, God of dreams. Makes perfect sense to me."

Making short work of what gods may or may not have been in the vision was the easy part. Trying to plan ahead for the coming days, well, that was a completely different animal. Nailing down the exact day, it seems, might have been made easier by Gus's attention to detail. Corn ready for harvest and shooting stars: all signs pointed to an October meteor shower. While the Orionids meteor shower could last the better part of a month, the peak of this celestial event was between the twenty-first and twenty-second of October.

Known the world over as being remnants of Halley's comet, this was a significant annual event. One could easily deduce it held some place in the hearts and minds of the gods; assuming they had hearts and minds. In any case, they had a target window to prepare for, though preparing for the actions of gods was a guessing game at best.

Everything seemed to make sense. Everything fell in line. The ancients coveted celestial events as well as any and all other signs from the gods. There would not be a time, at least to an agricultural society, that would hold more importance than the harvest.

"It just has to be this year," Citalli said. "It's not just your visions, Gus, but Canneo's as well. By all standards of the ancients he's already reached the age of manhood, though there's been no rite of passage performed."

"Is there a modern rite of passage?" Gus asked, "I mean, people these days just reach manhood through age. Not that I would want Canneo to be tried and tested, but it's a little sad that we no longer have to prove ourselves."

"I hear you, my man." Citalli replied, "There's really nothing that I know of in terms of a modern rite, and I grew up practicing many of the old ways. I think we should concentrate on what the proper method would be to honor and appease the gods. We've already ruled out bloodletting and ritualistic sacrifice. The ancients misinterpreted the anger of the gods as appeasement, don't want to make that mistake again."

Gus smiled and cracked a laugh, "Well, at least we know what not to do. I'm not sure if that qualifies as a starting point, but it does rule out the most violent avenue of approach."

"Fortunately for us, my mother taught me a little about non-violent tributes to the gods," Citalli said. "There were things such as obsidian, precious and semi-precious stones; sometimes these things would be crafted into jewelry. Harvested crops are always a good idea, and it will be the harvest."

Gus was well-versed in Mesoamerican folklore and knew the things Citalli mentioned were all ample gifts to the gods. Past ceremonies and traditions aside, the gods were coming for Canneo. Would gifts win the favor of the gods? Would they even be here for favor? Perhaps these questions would best be answered in dream; the types of dreams that tended to reveal themselves following dramatic visions. Maybe, just maybe, Canneo would start to have more detailed visions of the future.

In any case, the four of them, well, five if you counted Louie, had just a few short months to prepare. Gifts would need to be prepared and displayed, and Canneo's rite of passage would at least need to mimic some of the methods used by the elders. Furthermore, the group decided, they would steer clear of anything involving violent acts to man or beast; no blood, no infliction of death nor pain, nothing of the sort!

• • •

THE FOLLOWING MORNING THE ENTIRE FAMILY, GUS INCLUDED, began planting an additional garden just beside the cornfield. This garden would serve as a means to cultivate other crops, giving them a wider diversity of crops to offer the gods.

Because more crops planted meant more critters present, an additional scarecrow was created. Demanding the additional duty be assigned to him, Canneo was put in charge of scarecrow creation. Citalli purchased two dozen bales of hay from a neighboring farmer to give the area a certain feel of authenticity, he claimed the hay produced that "real farm" feeling. Canneo was given one of those bales to fashion his scarecrow.

"Any extra hay we'll spread it around these other bales," Citalli informed Canneo. "What do you think, son? Do you think this could pass as an authentic agricultural area?"

"If you say so, dad. I'm sure it looks nothing like what the elders had, but it sure looks like a small piece of heaven to me." Canneo smiled as grabbed his bale, made a silly lunge towards Louie to get him riled up, and darted off towards the house. "I'm going to create my masterpiece on the picnic table. Give a yell if you need me."

"He sure knows how to make an exit," Kara said. "That boy and that dog sure love the shade under that tree!"

"Probably a smart idea, girl. Gives him a table to work on, and gives Louie some softer grass to play in. My bet is that Louie moves over into the sun." Citalli reached his hand out as if to shake Kara's in a wager.

"Um, no. I know how much that dog loves to sunbathe! Maybe you could explain to me your plans for all of this hay. I know we settled on a couple dozen bales; but surely, you're not planning on just lining them up. I know you Citalli Patee, what's the plan?"

"Actually, Gus witnessed some hay thrown about parts of the area in a dream last night. Some was baled and some was scattered. In any case, we have a few months until harvest. I thought we'd let Gus figure that out as we go along. I mean, look at the guy! He's taking to farming like a fish to water, we may have to make him take a break." Citalli was amused, but serious about not letting Gus spend too much time working in the hot sun.

"When you're right, you're right," Kara said. She reached over and pinched the unsuspecting Citalli's ear. She gave it a playful tug and took off towards the crops Gus was sowing.

"Hey!" Citalli laughed as he gave chase. "Get back here, you!"

The two of them came running like teenagers towards an unsuspecting Gus. It can be difficult to hear what's coming in Oklahoma, the wind is constantly howling into your ears and teasing your eardrums.

Gus turned around just in time to see the two of them embrace in conclusion to a fun little game of chase. "What's this?" He said. "You two sure seem to have plenty of energy today!"

"The old man's lost a step, Gus!" Kara said jokingly, "I had to slow down and let him catch up!"

"Dream on girl, you know I've sneaky speed." Citalli, clearly out of breath, still had jokes.

"Gus," Kara said, "Citalli was worried you might need a break, but it looks like you're about done there."

"Yup, I'm finished. I think I missed my calling," Gus gave and exhaustive laugh. "It might be time we joined those two under the old maple, huh?"

"Let's do it," Citalli said, "and walk this time girly-girl!"

The trio made their way back to the house where Canneo was busily piecing together an impressive scarecrow. Kara fetched some iced tea and lemonade from the house, and the family enjoyed some together time under the tree. While they conversed and enjoyed some soothing and natural shade, Canneo finished his masterpiece and named it Sir Scares-a-lot.

CHAPTER 18

October 14, 2019

THE HEIGHT OF THE ANNUAL ORIONIDS METEOR SHOWER WAS BUT a week away, and Citalli and family hedged their bets on the notion that night would be the night. Prayer sessions with Citalli's mother and recent omens all pointed to the inevitable awakening of Cocijo.

Much like local Native American tribes, Mesoamerican peoples considered the owl to be a messenger. The sudden influx of owls in the area those past few weeks were coupled with the abrupt arrival of a bat colony, which gave further credence to the notion of an omen. Though no one could explain where such large numbers of these bats were coming from; it was largely attributed to the recent migrations of the monarch butterfly (also an omen). Be it superstition or omen, or that something was amiss.

Offerings may quell the fury of the gods, if fury was indeed in their hearts. Jewelry, locally made from turquoise and silver, highlighted a basket made from fresh cornhusks. Corn, peppers and legumes served as pillow-like fillers inside these baskets. Each basket was carefully arranged to be aesthetically pleasing and enriching to the very spirits that inhabited such divine beings.

Inanimate objects and foodstuff aside, the avarice of the gods desired the human conduit of the lightning god, called Canneo. Any other boy may have found himself afraid, nervous, or disconcerted; Canneo was none of these things. He seemed to relish the idea that the gods portrayed such warm-heartedness towards him. The very thought of being needed by the gods was intoxicating to Canneo, frightening to his mother and cautionary to both his father and godfather.

"One more time," Citalli turned to Gus, "you're sure he wasn't wearing anything special? Jeans and a t-shirt? Seems like he would wear something more, I don't know, ceremonial."

"Relax, Citalli," Gus started, "I'm sure they didn't come to see what the boy's fashion sense was like. I would imagine, if there's to be some sort of journey like we thought there would be, they would want him attired as any other youth. I say just let Canneo pick out his own clothes, this is his moment."

Staring down at the ground and nodding in approval, Citalli was barely capable of speech. Emotions sped their way through his mind, crippling him with feelings of joy, despair, sorrow and anger all at once. Maybe he was going insane or just mentally checking out until perception once again rejoined reality.

Moving up alongside him, Kara grasped his hand to comfort him. "What's that you two morons have been babbling on about for weeks? Control? It looks like the only one of us that's got any form of control is Canneo. He's controlling his emotions and embracing his part in all of this."

"And if we're leading him as a lamb to slaughter, baby?" Citalli asked. "What then? We lose our son for what? We're promised nothing upon Cocijo's return. The gods could judge favorably, disastrously, or not at all. We're basically walking into this blindfolded!"

"When we go to bed at night, do we know if we'll wake the next morning, Dad?" Canneo said, walking up behind them. "Have you ever gone into a day knowing exactly what would happen the next day? Not you Gus!" Canneo shot his clairvoyant godfather a wink. "Point is Dad, we walk through this life blindfolded, every minute of every day. For the first time in our lives, we know exactly what's going to happen. We know Cocijo will return from his sleep. That's enough for now, isn't it?"

"Told you," Kara said. "He's the only one of us making any sense. I gave up weeping over the unknown yesterday. Let's try to embrace the moment, accept we have no control over it, and just witness the most spellbinding and tantalizing moments in modern history. It's all we can do."

The three of them headed to the picnic table under the old maple for a final family meal before the anticipated event. Best to eat clean and traditional. Freshly grilled corn on the cob; still in the husk, of course. Grilled chicken, lightly seasoned with rosemary and various other herbs, and bread; simple bread just to help hold it all down.

As an ancient rite of passage into manhood for his son, Citalli was schooled through prayer on how to properly make an ancient and mystic tonic, more exactly, a tea. Similar to the tonics their ancestors made, this tonic would be made with peyote. Selected for its traditional uses by peoples native to the American continent, peyote seemed a safer choice than that of the jimson weed. While jimson weed, otherwise known as the devil's trumpet or moonflower, was a more powerful means of inducing visions, Citalli chose the peyote for its familiarity among the local native residents.

Peyote, a small cactus that grows in desert like areas, can still be dangerous and must be handled with care. Upon finishing their meal, the family each placed a small wedge of the cactus into their mouth. This ritual of chewing the peyote cactus is still practiced in parts of Mexico today, so Citalli, again deemed it safe enough in small quantities. The tea would be passed around the fire after sunset, causing further dilation of the pupils and leading to better night vision. Hopefully, everything was prepared and taken in small enough quantities so as to avoid hallucinations.

Feeling some fire in his blood and perhaps even some heart palpitations, Gus felt the need to talk it out a little. "Is anyone else feeling this peyote already? I feel heat, and my heart's running a little rapidly."

"Relax," Citalli said, "we've been over the side effects. Rapid heartbeat, awareness, clarity of thought and vision, but hopefully no one wigs out." Citalli was giggling almost uncontrollably as he attempted hide his sudden anxiety over the mescaline pumping through his veins.

"Well, I need to get up and move around," Kara said. "Can we go ahead and start that fire down by the pond? I think we may find the flames and heat a little soothing."

"Mom wins!" Announced Canneo. "That's what we need! We need a nice set of flames to watch while we wait to try dad's tea!"

Feeling like he could walk on air, Citalli agreed and got a nod of agreement from Gus. The wood for the fire was already dry, Gus and Citalli masterfully stacked it earlier in the day. The logs were placed over a bed of dried cornhusks and twigs, with more cornhusks and twigs woven between the logs. They weren't quite sure if this was the way the ancients did it, but it had seemed like a good idea at the time.

Canneo, the guest of honor, was handed a pack of wooden matches and given the duty of lighting the fire; the night's entertainment. A spark from a match, ignition of dried husks and within minutes they had a full-blown bonfire. The crackling of the fire made for a soothing addition to the silence of the night air.

Planning ahead, Canneo and his mother soaked some hay with water and covered it with blankets, placing their homemade bench far enough from the flames to ensure safety. Admiring their handiwork, the group sat down to enjoy the light show and await divine intervention.

The fire hissed and sang, flames danced and moved to the rhythmic vibrations of their natural environment, and that natural environment seemed to gain some sort of consciousness as if in a spell. Was it the peyote, or might their fire have actually come to life at the commands of the gods? It was a good question, but one whose answer would soon become irrelevant.

"Now, Citalli, I know you said the meteors are best viewed during the hours approaching dawn, but that doesn't mean they're going to wait that long, right?" Gus said. "I mean, it's barely gotten dark, I know that, but we could expect them at any time, right?"

"When you're right, you're right!" said Citalli, in his best English accent, "Fancy a spot of tea?" The competition was on as to whether the roar of the fire or the roar of laughter were louder.

Ceremoniously toasting to the health of one another, the group each took a small sip of the tea. The remnants of the tea were offered to the fire for approval. Fascinating, the water from the tea had no effect on the thundering flames.

Citalli glanced around at the group, "Man, we should have done this a long time ago. I feel so relaxed now. I can just imagine how our ancestors felt: watching the flames, dancing around them, bartering for the favor of the gods."

"Is that … I'm sorry, is that what you think we're doing?" Gus said, already stumbling over his words from the effects of the peyote. "Bartering for the favor of the gods? What, are we supposed to be trading some jewelry and … and maybe some maize for our future? We're back to control here Citalli, and there's no part of this we can possibly hope to control!"

"Ah, that's where you're wrong old man," Citalli shot back. "We're playing the influence game, and seeing if we can sway the gods into a favorable reaction." Citalli's pupils were dilated to such a degree that they reflected the fire like mirrors. "Thinking back to my army days, we taught that leadership was basically the art of influence. We influenced the soldiers through purpose, direction and motivation. Here, we're the soldiers! We influence the gods through obedience, offerings, and well, accountability."

As the hours passed the four of them found themselves getting quieter. Whether it was the effects of the mescaline-laden peyote, or just the anticipation of the inevitable, they sat speechlessly watching the fire. Louie was cuddled up on Canneo snoring up a storm, he sure seemed to dream a lot for a dog. He would often whimper or growl in his sleep, and it was always accompanied by some heavy breathing and restlessness. Tonight, was no different as he began breathing and growling in REM sleep before suddenly waking.

Clearly startled by his sudden jolt to consciousness, Louie looked around to see everyone laughing at his erraticism. His ears tucked back as he placed a silly look on his face by lifting the right side of his lip to show some teeth. He then jumped up and hoisted his butt in the air signaling his readiness to play. He and Canneo began to roll on the ground affectionately frolicking with one another.

As if still in dream, Louie suddenly stopped and ran towards the field of corn. He stopped and began barking at what appeared to be nothing but the night air. The scruff on the nape of his neck fired to attention as if jolted by static! There, right on cue, a shadow moved in from the still of the night.

Citalli's heart skipped a beat or three as he stood in an attempt to restrain Canneo. Paternal instinct kicked in and all he could think of was to protect the boy. Thinking better of the notion, he placed his arms around the boy. "I love you, son. Be strong!" A nod from the boy. "Are you sure you're ready for this?" Canneo said nothing but grabbed his father by the shoulder in silent affirmation.

Kara and Gus both rose to their feet and encouraged the boy forward, though he was already more than intent to go. It was all Kara could do to hold back her emotions and suppress tears, but Canneo needed strength, so he fought the urge to cry.

Canneo hushed Louie and began forward to the field they had decorated with baskets bearing gifts of tribute. The shadow seemed almost welcoming as the boy approached even closer; the brave garner respect from the gods. The shadow moved forward now, engulfing Canneo in its essence and guiding him onward to a suitable location where the boy's destiny awaited.

Canneo's movements were effortless now, each motion was summoned by a greater power, not just surrounding him but within him. The second figure advanced towards him now, presenting himself there just as Gus described, but even more powerful than words could describe. Gold mesh pelt, Headdress with feathers of jade, the light of electricity traveling through the headdress created by the golden ears of corn adorning the band of the headdress; it was Cozobi in all his magnificence.

The sky was clear, and an occasional meteor could be seen streaking across the sky as if being ridden by the spirits divinity. A clear sky with some faint lightning, Cocijo's awakening had begun. A crackle and a hiss from sheet lightning stretching outward across the sky, not a bolt wasted on earthly descent.

The fire abruptly hushed and sputtered, wilting as an autumn flower leaving naught but coals and murmuring light. A feeling of a supernatural vacuum overcame them as light began to shutter and ascend towards the heavens. They slowly moved forward, as the projection of the two figures faded to a dull glow. Forward towards Canneo.

There the boy lay, still and with eyes open, just as seen in Gus's vision. Also, as in Gus's vision, Louie was seated quietly by his side. In the vision Cozobi had been present, perhaps he only intended Gus to see him in vision, disallowing even a glimpse in material view.

They approached cautiously as one light, and one light only, was seen in its ascension back towards the heavens. As they neared the still body of Canneo a fog set in. At first, they thought it might be smoke from the burning coals of their fire, but it rapidly began to thicken and was odorless. They paused briefly before continuing forward. It felt as they were walking through water, each movement required more effort than the last. Pushing harder now, almost there … lights out.

• • •

THE FOUR OF THEM WERE NOT SURE IF DWELLING WITHIN A DREAM or trapped in reality when they awakened. The sky was freakishly aflame—orange and yellow dominated the night sky. Winds whipped and bats circled overhead as if in a feeding frenzy. The corn stalks were trampled down around them and there seemed to be nothingness beyond the boundaries of the cornfield.

Peering through the fiery skies now came a pair of black eyes, tinted in the most brilliant green. Series after series of incantations in a long-lost dialect ricochet from one eardrum to the next as if emitting from within their own minds. The chanting voices began to oscillate from a distance then close in, from a distance then close in; over and over mind-numbingly persistent.

Pecala, god of dreams ruled this realm. The dream was the reality and nothing else existed in that moment. The dream, and nothing. Those eyes, colder than steel, drew closer as if taking inventory of his entrapped guests. Citalli tried to speak, but made no sound. Louie's mouth and body moved in half-howl, half-bark; but not a peep could be heard.

Huddling together now, the group braced for whatever might come next. Canneo, up and standing beside his father now, reached down and picked up Louie in an attempt to calm him. They could feel a rush of cold followed by the singe of heat capturing them in a web of realization and enhancing some forbidden sense of calm.

Kneeling to appease the god of dreams, heads went down to look away from him and Louie was placed back on the ground; Canneo's hand rest on his scruff.

Feeling the dream god's acceptance of their obedience, a command was subliminally given for the subjects to raise their heads in submissive silence. The eyes drew closer and closer still until it felt as though the eyes were upon them, perhaps even among them.

A spear the length of a man with a gleaming, sharp obsidian tip was thrust from above them and planted itself at the edge of reality. A figure angrily moved from behind it and claimed the weapon. The figure was too distant to describe. Copijcha, God of war had joined the intervention.

An orb of brilliant light from a distance grew closer, then exploded in a powerful display of vigor. The light then took the shape of a human body and placed itself next to the war god, still naught but light. Cozobi placed himself beside the light god, creating an array of supernatural divinity that perhaps had never been seen by man, albeit in a sleep induced trance created by Pecala.

Behind the group, an array of what they understood to be lesser gods populated and filled the gaps of orange light between the greater gods. One god, of course, was missing: Cocijo, god of lightning and rain.

The ground began to shutter and quake. Cracks were visible and widening in front of them as a giant ball of fire struck in a violent and incapacitating manner. All sorts of rock and metallic debris scattered across the limited landscape as it became engulfed in fire. As the fire tempered and slowly subsided, the smoke cleared to reveal a large crater surrounding them. Canneo tapped his father on the shoulder and motioned. This, Citalli thought, was the crater in Canneo's dreams.

Centuries seemed to pass in minutes as the crater transformed from an impact cater, to a water filled basin, to a modern-day crevasse. Pine and oak trees surrounded and inhabited the area. This, no doubt, was their destination as selected by the gods. This is where the conduit, where Canneo, must be placed.

An image of Canneo lay in front of them in a small water filled fissure. *Strange*, Canneo thought, *to see himself.* The image showed a still Canneo with eyes opened and Citalli placing a Jade warrior's mask over his face. Then, standing and moving to his right, Citalli rushed over to join the images of the group atop the ridge. Missing nothing, this vision included Kara and Gus standing atop the ridge with Louie calmly seated next to Kara. Instructions were clear yet unspoken while leaving out one crucial piece of information: where was this crater?

The sky grew angry now, flashing with lightning and booming with thunder. The chanting within their heads grew louder, then louder still until it filled the canyon. All members of the animal kingdom scattered, something was coming. The lightning spread and joined, then spread and joined again, creating lightning bolts the size of legend, the size of godly power unseen for centuries. A single bolt of lightning thrust itself downward, and the blinding light of the gods was upon them.

Waking from their collective dream, they regained consciousness and found themselves lying under the autumn sun in Oklahoma. Each of them looked around baffled by the suddenness of waking. A moment or two of silent reflection was followed by nervous smiles and aching questions.

"So, I get it," Gus said, "but where's this crater? That sure didn't look like Oklahoma. Judging by the landscape, thickness of foliage and trees, I would say maybe somewhere out east."

"East sounds about right, I think," Citalli said. "I also have this premonition we'll be guided to the area."

Scratching his head and shooting an amused look Citalli's way, Gus replied, "And just how did you come up with that?"

"It's, uh, kinda the way of our people. What, you think we just charged blindly to sites we thought would appease the gods? Don't you think there was someone who had the ability and foresight to know the will of the gods. I believe we've identified our guide. That person, Gus, would be you, uija-tào."

"In my dreams," Gus began, "The shadow figure calls me that. He calls me uija-tào. I find myself wondering if I'm worthy of such a title."

"Gus, can't you see? You have the gift of foresight; you've witnessed the intentions of the gods. The gods speak to you and they call you uija-tào. Worthy, my friend, is not the word I would choose. If I had to choose a word, I would choose appointed."

CHAPTER 19

October 20, 2019
In route from Oklahoma eastward

GOOD THING GUS RENTED A VAN UPON HIS ARRIVAL TO OKLAHOMA, Citalli's car was no longer reliable enough for the cross-country trip. With the peak of the Orionids happening on the twenty first of October, the newly minted uija-tào set the travel start date for the day before. Citalli and family were calling him uija-tào so much even he was beginning to embrace it. Maybe his adoption and subsequent education could all be attributed to some high level plan the gods had in place for him all along.

Planning on traveling straight south from Taugui, Gus was thumbing through a road atlas. Technology aside, printed road atlases just tended to give old timers a better feel for the road, especially since all they really knew was that they were headed east. "Well, looks like we should head down to Dallas and hang a left. Interstate twenty headed east is our path," Gus announced.

"And then?" Citalli shot back, "Any idea where this crater is yet? I mean, there's quite a few meteor craters we know about. Heck, there might even be a few we don't know about. In any case, looks like its not just east, but southeast!"

Gus began to think about how in the world this huge event took place last week and nobody noticed. Putting aside the obvious fact that the majority of the action happened in a dream world created by Pecala, and you'd still have questions surrounding all those flying critters. Owls and bats along with a slew of flying insects would not be so easily ignored by the indigenous population. These were signs of omens north and south of the border. Many ancient civilizations worldwide considered these flying creatures as omens. Modern civilizations tended to lose their connection with nature, believing creatures of the animal kingdom to be spiritless.

"Where are those two at?" Kara said. "Canneo! Louie! We're ready to go, get the lead out!"

It appeared as though the two decided to make one last jaunt out to the cornfield, and of course, they had to stop and skip a few stones at the pond. They came running up side by side, playfully taking short lunges at one another. "Coming, mom," Canneo yelled. "We just wanted to grab a couple of pieces of home with us before we left."

Holding a plastic grocery bag in each hand, Canneo showed off a few husks of ripe and ready corn in one and some random pieces from the corn stalks in the other.

"What are the corn stalks for?" Citalli asked

"In my vision I saw them around me. Not sure if they're some form of offering or just for decoration, but I saw them," the boy answered.

Louie and Canneo then jumped into the third row of seats in the van, prime real estate for sleep and play. Kara took a seat in the middle row, while Gus and Citalli occupied the front. Everybody buckled in, except Louie, and down the road they went. Kara reminded the two men she would own a third of the driving, not a request!

Making good time, the fully occupied van whisked through Oklahoma, Texas and Louisiana, stopping only once for gas just outside Dallas. Approaching the Mississippi river at the state line Kara, who was now driving, announced the mighty river.

"Can we stop?" Canneo asked. "Me and Louie both need to pee anyway."

"Sure, Let's just cross over to the Mississippi side first." Kara said as she shook Citalli to wake him. "We're going to stop and get some air. I thought we could find a spot to walk along the river's edge."

Gus seemed to wake as she woke Citalli. He concurred stretching their legs would be a good thing. Besides, not many rivers on earth could move a person's soul like the Mississippi.

After parking the van, they began making their way to the water's edge. Canneo was reminded not to let Louie too close to the water's edge, currents could be strong and whisk the little rascal away. Making their way out of the van, they plopped themselves down a good ten feet away from the bank. Louie didn't really appreciate being on a leash, but it was for his own good.

They stretched while Louie and Canneo rolled in the grass uninhibited by onlookers watching. A boy and his dog, who couldn't appreciate that? All the same, they had journeyed far enough for one day.

"What say we stop and get a couple of rooms for the night?" Gus said to the weary group. "One for me, and one for you three. Sound like a plan?"

"I think you were reading my mind, Gus." Citalli stretched like an old man needing a work over. "Kara, I don't suppose you could find a pet friendly hotel on that gizmo of yours, could you?"

Rolling her eyes a bit at Citalli's lack of proficiency with technological devices she answered, "Sure babe, no problemo!"

The group settled on a simple, but safe little motel just off the beaten path, Tranquil Forest Inns. Meager accommodations at a modest price, the motel had everything they needed: beds and cable TV. Checking in was a snap, and they were able to get adjoining rooms, though Gus felt the need to keep the adjoining door closed for privacy.

Citalli decided now would be a good time for the two men to have a sit down and discuss the coming day's events. Since Gus was actually appointed uija-tào by the gods and not just by Citalli, he would need his rest later in order to interpret the will of the gods and choose the proper location. Best just to settle for a six-pack of brew and leave the remainder of the peyote in his bag. They had just enough of the mystical cactus left to make a few wedges for the awakening, and Citalli had a feeling they would need it to calm their nerves.

A drumroll knock on the door prompted a smiling welcome from Gus. "I was wondering who was buying the beer tonight," he said.

"You know me," Citalli answered with a smirk. "At first, I thought the beer may be inappropriate, but then that *what if* feeling hit me kinda hard. What if this is our last chance to share a beer together?" The two men shared a chuckle as Citalli made himself at home in Gus's room. "Just do me a favor, no talking until your third beer."

"That's a deal," Gus said popping the top and washing back the first sip.

True to his word, Gus polished off his first two beers in silence, then popped the top off the third one and began. "You know, tomorrow's going to be unpredictable at best, don't you?"

"Now what makes you say that?" He had Citalli at a little bit of a loss. "We all witnessed the same thing in Pecala's dream world, Gus. I mean sure, we don't know the final destination yet, but we know the end game, don't we?"

"Do we?" Gus seemed concerned. "My vision from last night showed everything that would happen today, and I mean showed it exactly how it happened. But, tomorrow, that's a whole different ball of wax, a whole different enchilada."

"Now you're making me hungry," Citalli said, always the joker. "But really, if everything today was so precise, man, I guess I just don't get it."

"Look, we're awakening the most powerful god of the Zapotec empire tomorrow; and in case you didn't notice, the dream ended with a bright flash of light from a massive lightning bolt. We have no idea what happens next. For all we know, it could be the end of the world we're seeing."

"Come on Gus! Don't be so pessimistic! Why would the gods, all of them, present themselves to us just to destroy us? Listen, we're all nervous, we're all scared, but this is historic! Of course, if you told anyone you were in contact with ancient Zapotec deities, you'd be in a strait jacket tomorrow." *As funny as that is*, Citalli thought, *it's probably true.*

"Whatever happens, we're in it together," Gus said. "Now, lets get some rest. I would say we have a big day ahead of us tomorrow, but that would be the understatement of a lifetime."

"Dude … just … dude …" That was all Citalli had, as close to speechless as it got. It was a hot ticket, no doubt about that. "Gus, I'm glad you're here, I'm glad you came along; heck, I'm glad you're guiding us, we'd be lost without you. Just one request for tomorrow, huh? Please try to keep some positive vibes. Now, I'm out … see you in the A.M."

CHAPTER 20

The Awakening

AWAKENING DAY WAS FINALLY HERE. DRIVING MOST OF THE DIS-
tance needed the previous day, there was ample opportunity
to sleep in a little; besides, the awakening was clearly going to be
at night. With sleep came dream, with dream came vision, and
with vision came the last two pieces of the puzzle. Piece one: their
destination was an impact crater site on the outskirts of the city
of Wetumpka, Alabama. Piece two: the jade warrior's mask would
be delivered to the site of the ritual by none other than Copijcha,
the god of war.

Brunch would be the proper term for the first activity of the
day, at a time Canneo and his mother identified as "tennish". Unlike
before the previous ritual, there were no rules set for today's meal.
Eat what makes you happy. Since this would be the last official
sit-down meal, the group decided to just snack on various tidbits
for the rest of the day. Citalli's best guess was that the majority of
them would struggle with appetite later due to nervousness. All
except Canneo and Louie, those two could eat anytime, anyplace,
and just about any thing.

Stopping at a little Mom and Pop's diner in Vicksburg named
Pauly Possum's Last Stand seemed to be as good an idea as any.

The name was clearly poking fun at the fact that some of the area's inhabitants still made a meal of the ghostly looking little varmint, while embracing the rich history of Vicksburg as a Civil War battlefield. Canneo chose the spot because the name of the diner amused him, and any diner with a name like that probably wouldn't mind preparing a plate for Louie; albeit Louie would have to eat outside.

"Waitress, the possum tail grits don't have real possum in them, do they?" Citalli asked, looking at a menu filled with puns designed to humor their guests with visions of what one might call back woods cuisine.

Letting out a little giggle, "No sir, if you flip the menu over there's a more appealing description of the meals on the back. Sorry, I guess I should've mentioned that."

The young lady was all of about seventeen-years old and carried a beautifully fair skin tone that complimented her long, wavy blonde locks. She stood about Canneo's height and wore cut off denim shorts and a plain white t-shirt. Speaking of Canneo, the boy had gone into a silent blush and was quite smitten by the pretty young lady who possessed what people in the area referred to as southern charm.

Possum tail grits translated to grits with bacon strips, they apparently used thin strips of bacon to give the appearance of tails; just for kicks of course. Citalli and Kara both decided to have the grits, Citalli would add a side of scrambled eggs, while Kara preferred over easy. Coffee and avocado toast named the possum vomit plate, which was Gus's breakfast of choice. All Canneo could manage to spit out was, "Pancakes, please," while trying to maintain his cool. A side of critter cakes (sausage patties) was ordered as a to-go order for Louie.

"Eat up Canneo," his mother said, "and put your tongue back in your mouth." Kara was clearly amused by her son's bashful nature. True to form, Canneo nodded and dug in.

Citalli took a break form shoveling grits to defend the young man. "Come on girl, you know how speechless you were when you met me. Clearly the boy takes after his mother."

"Yeah, we know who the nervous one was, and it sure wasn't me," she whipped back.

"Finally!" Citalli said, slapping the table with an open palm. "After all these years, you finally admit you were the aggressor!"

Gus reached for a napkin as his laughter caused coffee to spew from his nose, "Man that burned!" He let out. "I would call it a waste of coffee, but Kara, you walked right into that!"

The group enjoyed a laugh at Kara's expense, though Canneo innocently fixed those mahogany eyeballs on the young waitress. Catching on to his obvious interest, she smiled flirtatiously at her admirer; Canneo was a good-looking young man, and innocence was always in vogue.

Polishing off brunch and turning to Citalli for shop talk, Gus had the reliable atlas in his hands. "Wetumpka, Alabama," he started out, pointing at the page, "that's where we're headed. I've already entered it into the GPS in the van, looks to be about five hours away. That'll give us enough time to perform a quick once over of the place before dark."

Kara quickly pulled up the city of Wetumpka on her cell phone. "Says here it's the city of natural beauty. Do you think they have any idea what's coming?"

"Not a chance," Citalli said, "no way. I guess that's a good thing, wouldn't want a panic on our hands now, would we?"

"I guess not," Gus said. "We should probably be on our way. Canneo, last call for ogling, ha-ha! If it's meant for us to come back this way, then we'll stop here again, and you can hit her with some pick-up lines."

Grinning with embarrassment Canneo took that part serious, "Careful Gus, I'm going to have to quote you on that! If I can muster up enough courage to get me through tonight, there's no way I strike out after that! No way!"

Laughing sheepishly, Citalli swung his arm over Canneo's shoulder, "See there, Gus, the boy's a Patee. The same animal magnetism that drew his mother to me is going to win the heart of that pretty little thing right there. Bet on it!"

"Getting deep in here, babe. Good thing I wore my boots today!" Kara shot back. They all had on some manner of hiking boots for the rugged terrain. Besides the fact it was an impact crater and they had never been there before, there would obviously be buckets of rain coming when Cocijo arrived.

Leaving payment and a nice tip at the table, Canneo gave a last glance at the waitress before heading outside. She threw him a wink, "Name's Melodie, by the way. I'll see you when you get back," she smiled and winked again.

Whoops, she obviously overheard that part of the conversation. Oh well, no doubt that would help break the ice a little if and when they got back. Canneo thought. "So, it's a date then?" Pushing his luck seemed like the right thing to do in the moment.

"Yup," she said. "How could I say no to those eyes? But, yeah, as long as you're buying the pizza dinner, it's a date."

Canneo smiled politely, nodded and waved. He was bursting with excitement and anticipation on the inside, cool as a cucumber on the outside. Funny what a little success will do to a young man's confidence. As he walked, seemingly on air to the car, he met the three grinning faces of his biggest fans. While Louie inhaled his breakfast, Canneo shot the group a nod displaying his achievement; no words spoken.

Citalli assigned himself driving duties for the day; after all, five hours was nothing compared to the day before. Kara sat shotgun so Gus could assemble his thoughts and visions in the second row. Louie and Canneo once again jumped in the back and nodded off into a blissful and silent sleep.

After a solid five hours of driving they arrived safely just outside of Wetumpka, at a historic site named Fort Toulouse-Fort Jackson. The site was chosen by Gus, not because of its historical significance, but because of its close proximity to Wetumpka and its relative remoteness.

Sitting comfortably along the shores of the Coosa River, the camp grounds of the park offered a quiet, scenic area to relax and prepare for the night's events. Because the actual sites of Fort Toulouse and Jackson had long since been abandoned, the structures in the fort were recreations of a time almost forgotten. Apparently, the French discovered the area referred to as Fort Toulouse in the year 1717, but try telling this to the Creek Indians who had already inhabited the region for generations. In any case, camping season was almost over and the park's few remaining tenants were relishing the last few days of serenity.

"Why don't we just stretch out a little, maybe take a stroll along the river?" Citalli said, taking in a deep breath of fresh air. "There's still plenty of daylight left to check out the crater. What say, I don't know, thirty minutes?"

"Sounds good to me," Gus answered. "It's beautiful here, really, I can see why the Creek, and of course European forces, chose this area. Great water supply right next to the river, fertile soil for planting crops, and I bet the hunting and fishing were really something back in those days."

Citalli looked at Gus a little coy and shot back, "The hunting and fishing here are still really something. But I guess I know what you're saying. With so few people compared to today, wildlife had to have been abundant."

They walked around for a while, Louie was back on the leash he found less than desirable, but at least they weren't cooped up in that van. As they admired the natural beauty still surrounding the area, Citalli went ahead and rationed out the last few wedges of the peyote cactus. "Just slap it in your mouth, nibble and suck on the juices for a while. Try to make it last a while," he said. "I'll wait until we get on site for my peyote, no excuses for driving impaired."

By the time they made a quick jaunt around the area their thirty minutes had elapsed, and it was time to jump back in the van. Just a short drive this time, according to Gus about ten minutes driving with another ten minutes walking.

Driving into the outskirts of town, there was a large Creek nation casino on the left, and almost directly across the street were a couple of pharmacy stores. No doubt this was meant to be the spot, casino or no casino. Indigenous lands along the outer edges of the impact crater, sounded like divine providence to Citalli.

Just as planned, they parked at the first of the pharmacies, then proceeded to walk east into the pit carved by the meteor. While walking, Citalli placed the last wedge of mystical cactus into his mouth, the zesty taste of the mescaline tingled his senses. He couldn't help but to wonder if the elders of the indigenous felt powers emanating from the crater, or maybe just ended up here by chance.

The crater was a miracle of the natural world. Huge cliffs of white and yellowed earth were formed and sharpened by the meteor much as one would sharpen obsidian blades. Aside from the lack of a glassy shine, that's exactly how Citalli viewed them.

The exact spot where Canneo was to be placed had not yet been revealed, but Gus assured the group they would know in due time. The vision they were all granted by Pecala showed a fissure, slightly filled with water, the vast gouges cut into the earth made it possible for that to be just about anywhere in this area. Clouds were quickly forming, and moisture hung in the air. Rain and darkness would reveal the exact location shortly.

Gus, almost mesmerized by the manner in which the clouds were moving in, began to scan the immediate area. "I think we should head up there on that ridge! Not quite sure that's the exact ridge we're supposed to be on, but those clouds look like they mean business. I'm also guessing that we're not waiting until nightfall. Kinda looks like our entrance to the crater may have kicked things off."

"High ground it is!" Claimed Citalli with a firm voice and a playful expression. The peyote helped keep him calm with a side of silly in the face of what was coming.

Walking around the razor-sharp edges instead of attempting to scale them, the group made it atop the ridge and under the cover of trees. Winds began to howl as pine needles escaped their branches and descended towards the ground. Moisture turned to sprinkle, and sprinkle to rain, the darkness of night was early and ominous.

Ravens alighted in the trees as if calling them to wake. Deer retreated, scampering off into dark forests of pine, oak and hickory. As the brief downpour came to a sudden halt, birds of prey circled the area, mimicking the dream and calling to the heavens.

From the center of the airborne phenomenon shone a dull-green light that grew and brightened. Shining, twisting and reaching for the ground, the light shimmered and glistened the deepest green; green to match that of the lights in Pecala's eyes. This, however, was no dream.

Positive the moment of truth had arrived, Canneo turned to his mother and placed a kiss on her cheek. "Hold onto that for me," he said in a half whisper.

Louie smartly maneuvered his way backwards as Kara threw herself into her boy's already open arms. "I'll return that kiss as soon as we're done here. I love you, Canneo." She was done holding back tears. Tears which were gently wiped away by her son.

"The light!" Gus yelled to Citalli, "the light, it carries the mask! Take Canneo to the light!"

Handing Louie's leash to his mother with the embrace of a fully-grown man, Canneo turned to his father. Words were lost and useless. A hundred times over, expressions of love filled the space between them; no need for that today. Citalli grabbed his son by the back of the head and pulled him into his shoulder as Canneo formed a reassuring fist and rested it upon his father's chest.

Turning and nodding, the two gestured their goodbyes to Kara and Gus while Louie's front legs were already resting on Canneo's thighs; his ears were pinned back, and his tail was still. Canneo reached down to give his friend a loving pat on the back followed by a kiss on the crown of the head. One last smile and they headed towards the beam of light.

Along the jagged gouges that decorated the floor of the crater, rainwater pooled. The water formed ripples from the trembling ground as if rejoicing in the return of the lightning god. The beam of light pulsed and flickered as it detached itself from the jade object gleaming from beneath the water. Wind traveling through the crevasses pushed Citalli and Canneo back as the mask beckoned them forward.

"Lean into it son, Lean!" Citalli yelled as if he were still the sergeant guiding soldiers. *Too tired on a road march, lean into it. Too tired on a run, lean into it.* Locking shoulders to combine strength, they hunkered over at the waist and drove their feet into the jagged stone beneath them. "Push! Lean! We're almost there, dig deep!"

The harder they pushed, the lower they leaned; nearly on all fours they finally reached the mask. Pure jade, the mask shined with screaming glory as it glared fury from its eyes. As they looked into the eyes of the mask, it appeared to stare back; yellow eyes radiating the eminence of the sun. Canneo, accepting commands from within himself, lie on his back, placing his head beside the waiting warrior's mask.

Citalli picked up the mask, its weight requiring both hands. "Ready, Canneo? I said, are you ready?"

Canneo's eyes were open but he heard nothing and looked only upward—upward to the heavens, to the source of the commands pulsing through his body. Citalli looked up to Gus, questioning what came next, to which Gus motioned back to place the mask on Canneo. Abruptly the wind stopped as the mask pulled itself towards the entranced boy. Citalli guided it in an attempt to gently rest it atop Canneo's face.

Citalli heard a sizzling hiss from above and looked to the sky. Lightning to consumed the sky spreading like cracks in ice and crackling like bones breaking in the great beyond. Leaving his son's side as commanded by Pecala in dream, he made his way to the top of the ridge, planting himself between Kara and Gus.

The skies were alive with energy from massive bolts of lightning searing through the night sky almost singeing the funneling clouds above them. The clouds rolled and tinted the skies orange then red, antagonizing the beams of light, enraging the charged particles.

A bolt of lightning fired downward from the heavens beyond the clouds, widening as it stretched towards the ground. Ceasing its advance some fifty feet from landfall a figure of sorts appeared at its base and widened, then elongated and formed facial features: eyes, ears, mouth, nose, all pure lighted energy. From this head exploded the neck and shoulders from which extremities splintered from the discharge, landing feet that exploded the rocky surface of the crater on contact.

As the figure continued to grow and form, arms detonated from the shoulders and hands reached angrily at the sky. Roaring and screaming dominated the landscape, the earth beneath them boomed, beaten like a drum as Cocijo advanced. Boom! Boom! Boom! His feet crafted from lightning bolts pounded the ground, punished anything beneath them until finally; finally, the figure stopped before them.

Fifty-feet of glimmering, crackling lightning in the shape of a giant, his eyes fixated on a familiar landscape with an equally unfamiliar civilization built amongst it. The figure looked back to the sky, as bolts of lightning struck the giant provoking bellowed howls of fury. Clenching fists of pure energy the figure roared towards the sky, consuming every last discharge of radiation from the storm; the presence of reassembled divinity stood before them.

Cocijo stared commanding obedience from the onlookers who knelt in fear and astonishment, fixated on this colossal presence before them. Extending a single static-charged arm, Cocijo flicked and waved his palm commanding the body of Canneo to levitate before him. Canneo, surrounded in a field of pure white lightning, returned growls of ire with fists clenched together and head bowing in a stance of submissive veneration.

Cocijo spun the levitating body of Canneo around inspecting his newly acquired disciple, the boy firmly held his stance. He guided the body of the young man in circles and slowly returned him back to solid ground. As Canneo made contact with the freshly crushed rubble and debris dancing atop the rumbling rock of the crater he assumed a kneeling position, head remaining at a bow.

The storm within the god was calmed by Canneo's essence, as he recognized a descendant of his divinity. Thundering skies grew silent while vibrations of the earth grew still, a moment of peaceful tranquility suppressing the turmoil from within the storm. Then, in an instant, catapulted from the crater, a single beaming lightning bolt returned to the heavens.

Awake and aware, Cocijo returned to the realm of the gods.

CHAPTER 21

W EEPING TEARS OF JOY, KARA LET LOOSE LOUIE'S LEASH FREEING him. Down from the ridge and through newly crumbled earth at top speed, Louie sped his way to Canneo, three slow humans in tow. Exhausted, Canneo still knelt on one knee, until Louie arrived and leapt to knock him backwards. As his back slammed to the ground, the jade mask detached from his face and landed on the soil behind him.

"Louie!" Smiling and laughing, Canneo tried to hug the hound; Louie, more interested in soaking Canneo's face with dog slobber, licked him frantically. "Easy, buddy, easy!" He could barely speak through his own buoyant laughter.

Citalli, Kara and Gus cast aside all manner of composure, joining the two playmates on the ground and nestling in a frenzied family embrace. Tears, laughter, hugging, kissing; nothing else mattered in this moment, nothing!

"Baby, I was so scared! I prayed and I prayed that he wouldn't tear you apart!" Kara said, pulling Canneo to rest her cheek upon his, squeezing and inundating her boy with affection. "As promised," she whispered in his ear as she lovingly placed that kiss back upon his cheek.

"Don't let go," Canneo whispered to his mother, "not yet." He sunk his forehead into her shoulder, feeling safety in his mother's arms like a newborn babe. Weeping tears of joy and feeling a new-found inner peace, Canneo was reborn, a man.

Citalli and Gus felt the sudden urge to inspect the warrior's mask not two feet away, where it had fallen from Canneo's face. Amazingly, there wasn't a scratch on it. Its brilliant shine flickered and radiated in the moonlight of the now clear skies.

"Humph, not a scratch!" Gus said in amazement. "Not a single, solitary scratch. Almost like it's never been touched."

"I believe that's a sign," Citalli said.

Looking perplexed and shooting Citalli a whimsical glare, Gus shook his head, "Now you're interpreting signs? Lightning hit you in the head when I wasn't looking?"

Grinning like a child with shiny new toy Citalli rose an eyebrow, "After all these years, you don't believe me? I'm telling you, this is a sign."

"Can't wait to hear this one, Citalli. OK, let me have it. What's this sign?"

Politely removing the mask from Gus's hands and looking back towards the rest of the family, "I believe this is a sign that we should get the heck out of here!" Pushing the mask forward in a stopping motion, "Hear me out, just hear me out. We're obviously on someone's land; city, state or private citizen, this land belongs to someone."

Canneo stood and helped his mother to her feet. Kara, seizing the opportunity, replied to her husband's proclamation to Gus. "I believe he's got a point, Gus, right there on top of his head!"

Laughter ensued from the group as they continued to recover emotionally and reclaim their senses. Citalli passed the mask to Canneo, "Here, son. This belongs to you. You earned it." Giving his son a hug that ended in a headlock, "Besides, I thought you wanted to go back to Vicksburg!"

With all the excitement Canneo almost forgot his promised date, pizza dinner with Melodie. "Hold on, someone's going to have to come up with some scratch so I can pay for dinner. I mean, Louie doesn't look to have any money on him, so we're down to you three! It might be a good idea if you all chip in, you know what they say about first impressions, of course."

Kara placed her arm around Canneo, "You already made that impression, son. It's obvious she's into you. All the same, you can write me and your dad down for fifty bucks; and no, that's not negotiable! Well, unless you want to negotiate for less."

"Fifty bucks?!" Citalli said clownishly, "I was thinking triple figures! Fifty each, and this is me putting my foot down, girl." Citalli stomped his foot playfully as if literally putting it down.

"I was thinking," Gus said, slapping Canneo on the back, "You did do the lion's share of the work. Put me down for fifty!" Sneering now at Citalli, "As much as it pains me to admit it, your father has a legitimate point. It's not just that we're obviously on someone's property, no-no-no. That astronomically huge event that just permeated through the entire cosmos is going to attract attention, a lot of attention."

"See," Citalli said, "had to put my foot down again! Let's put that mask in my backpack, huh? I really don't think it would be a great idea to let anyone see that."

"Twice in one day he's right!" Kara proclaimed. "Your dad's right twice in one day! That usually means rain's coming, but I think we already had that one covered."

They made their way through the debris, cautiously moving with a purpose. They visually scanned the area, dumbfounded in amazement over the trampled remains of the heavily wooded area. Canneo remarked on how the crater was once again visible from a distance giving the group a chuckle. And Louie? He pulled on the leash again, pulling until he almost choked himself.

"We need to ditch this collar and get him a harness," Canneo said. "A country dog like Louie just isn't built for wearing a collar; know what I mean?"

Gus looked sideways at Citalli, "This actually does look to qualify for animal cruelty, poor thing's choking himself."

"Dude," Citalli started, "don't let Louie hear you call him an animal, he's my youngest son. Shortest too, ha-ha!"

Louie looked back for approval, or was it hunger? In any case, Louie looked back on the four of them and pulled forward towards the van that was now in sight. Just as Gus was hoping, the van was intact with barely a scratch on it. The entire city, for that matter, seemed to be intact.

Upon reaching the van, they turned and viewed the fallen forest entrance. Looking around, it became clear that the only area affected was that of the impact crater. Climbing back into the van it was decided that a quick get away would be the preferred action as they could hear the sirens approaching.

Out of the parking lot and onto the highway, they headed out of town leaving the city of Wetumpka in the rearview mirror. They headed south, then west, on the road that would eventually take them home.

AUTHOR'S NOTE

SOME OF THIS BOOK IS LOOSELY BASED ON WHAT WE CONSIDER fact today, but by no means is this meant to be a history of the Zapotec peoples; the book is fiction and should be considered as such. The Zapotec are still with us today, and I can only hope this book brings some recognition to the cloud people. I hope one day we can shift our focus away from their violent past that tends to dehumanize them. If we find the ability to do so, we'll find a people that believed and loved as fiercely as any civilization the world has known.

Much of what we know about the ancient Zapotec is a mixture of historical records written by the Spaniards, and what we have learned through discovery of ancient cities and artifacts. Sadly, Spaniards destroyed most of the written histories recorded by Mesoamerican cultures, leaving us with less than accurate depictions of these ancient cultures. My passion for self-study of Mesoamerican cultures led me to fashion this story.

All of the characters in this book are fictional except one: Louie. The Beagle, Louie, joined my family shortly after my diagnosis of cancer. The cloud of depression consumed me upon my diagnosis of this disease. Louie's gentle nature gave me the ability to smile again. It is for this reason that I have decided to share a small piece of him with any and all who thumb through these pages.

Besides Louie, there are some other fun facts in the book including the deities depicted in the book, which are perhaps the most widely recognized Zapotec gods. Though we do know the ancient name of the City of Mitla was indeed Lyobaa, we do not know what the city of Monte Albàn was called by its indigenous inhabitants.

Not all of the fictional characters in this book had meanings associated with their names, but some names were derived from Mesoamerican languages:

Ayotli (also spelled Ayohtli)	Turtle
Beedxe'	Jaguar
Cayo	Rooster
Citalli (also spelled Citlalli)	Star
Canneo	Birth of water
Danaà	Stream
Ikal	Spirit
Kabil	He who has a good hand to sow
Kasakir	Daybreak
Zyanya	Always/Forever

There were also two fictional locations in the book. First: Beyulu, Florida is a play on the word Biulu', meaning hummingbird. The second: Taugui, as stated in the book means sitting outside … this was the only word taken from the Kiowa/Apache.

The inspiration behind using the meteor impact crater in Wetumpka, Alabama was simple: Wetumpka is my hometown and

I am a proud graduate of Wetumpka High School. Fort Toulouse-Fort Jackson was used for its historical value, as were the mentions of the Creek people who inhabited those lands.

ACKNOWLEDGMENT

I would like to thank my editor Amber Byers of Tadpolepress.com for her spot-on corrections. The guidance provided was delivered to me in an extremely professional manner and resulted in a book of which I am extremely proud.

A special thank you to Sue Campbell for the design and production of *Awakening Cocijo*. An absolute joy to work with and a true professional!

ABOUT THE AUTHOR

THOMAS (TOM) JUAREZ IS A RETIRED UNITED STATES ARMY SOLDIER with about twenty-one years of active federal service. Hailing from Wetumpka, Alabama, Tom currently enjoys his military retirement with his wife in Sterling, Oklahoma. Tom is pictured here with his beagle, Louie, who was adopted into the Juarez family following Tom's successful treatment of cancer.

If you enjoyed this book please consider leaving a review on the site where you purchased it. Even just a few words make all the difference to an author's success.

CONTACT THE AUTHOR:

t tom-juarez.tumblr.com ✉ tjuarez66@yahoo.com

Made in the USA
Columbia, SC
27 May 2019